A DRUM THUDDED ONCE, STARTLING HIM.

The priest plunged his knife over the captive's head and into his breast. Blood sprang forth, crimson in the shifting spotlights, and the priest made a sidelong slashing incision from which, dropping the knife, he pulled out the victim's miraculously living heart. . . . The heart, held up, glistened and beat—*pa-pum, pa-pum, pa-pum*—like a flayed baby rabbit. Then the priest whirled away, the tom-tom mocking the beat of an adrenaline-fed human heart.

Feeling an instinctive horror and revulsion, Lucian sat in the elegant supper club and watched the actors mime the ancient rite.

The Latest Science Fiction and Fantasy
From Dell Books

HEALER *by F. Paul Wilson*

WE WHO ARE ABOUT TO . . . *by Joanna Russ*

THE SILVER WARRIORS *by Michael Moorcock*

DEUS IRAE *by Philip K. Dick and Roger Zelazny*

YLANA OF CALLISTO *by Lin Carter*

FLASHING SWORDS! #4:
BARBARIANS AND BLACK MAGICIANS
edited by Lin Carter

SUNSTOP 8 *by Lou Fisher*

GORDON R. DICKSON'S SF BEST

THE OPHIUCHI HOTLINE *by John Varley*

A WREATH OF STARS *by Bob Shaw*

KEEPERS OF THE GATE *by Steven G. Spruill*

SPACE WAR BLUES *by Richard A. Lupoff*

Books by Michael Bishop:

A FUNERAL FOR THE EYES OF FIRE

UNDER THE SHATTERED MOONS

A LITTLE KNOWLEDGE

STOLEN FACES

FACES

Michael Bishop

A DELL BOOK

Published by
DELL PUBLISHING CO., INC.
1 Dag Hammarskjold Plaza
New York, N.Y. 10017

Dell ® TM 681510, Dell Publishing Co., Inc.

ISBN: 0-440-18328-6

Reprinted by arrangement with
Harper & Row, Publishers, Inc.

Printed in the United States of America

First Dell printing—July 1978

For Jeri & Jamie & Stef & the house
in Pine Mountain

More than once during these three months he asked himself: "Am I mad that I see what others do not, or are they mad who do these things that I see?" Yet they (and there were so many of them) did what seemed so astonishing and terrible to him, with such quiet assurance that what they were doing was necessary, and was important and useful work, that it was hard to believe they were mad; nor could he—conscious of the clearness of his thoughts—believe he was mad. This kept him in a continual state of perplexity.

Tolstoi, *Resurrection* (1899)

CONTENTS

STOLEN
FACES

ONE

Troika at the
Sancorage

On his second morning as kommissar of the Sancorage complex on Tezcatl, the "lepers" brought Yeardance their god.

When the shaveskull apprentice came up behind his desk and touched him on the shoulder, he had been thinking of St. Croix rum and the instant of slip-fix. He'd also been thinking, for reasons that were unclear to him, of Jaeger, his birth planet. Lucian Yeardance had been recently demoted, all the way from a shipboard astrogation-and-engineering position to this anonymous kommissariat on Tezcatl. Although he wasn't bitter, he was sick of Komm-service wrangles and bewildered by his new responsibilities. He was weary of petty evil. A year short of fifty, he knew that he wouldn't survive many more such politically motivated off-shuntings, but he still didn't intend to cry mercy of the system that had dropped him here.

" 'Sar Yeardance," said the shaveskull Gaea, a girl of fourteen, "from the Compound, a troika."

"Here?"

"Coming, sir."

"So soon?"

"Ebarres didn't have them served yesterday, sir, and it was time for our weekly run. The rule is, if the run

is missed, they may come to the Sancorage and visit
the med-kommissar. The Long Quarantine confines
them only to the Tezcatlipoca Reserve, sir, not just to
their village."

"But yesterday, Gaea, Neo-starb Zobay, I arrived.
Yesterday, Ebarres left." A man very glad to be going,
Ebarres. Already packed when Yeardance arrived,
Ebarres had shaken hands, wished his replacement
well, and departed for the Town Tezcatl light-probe
port a hundred kilometers northwest of the Reserve.
He had gone off in a troika, and no one had accompa-
nied him. That was the way he had seemed to want it.

"Aye, sir, that's true," Gaea Zobay said. "But still
they come."

"Well, should I meet them?"

"They *will* be met, 'Sar Yeardance. I fear they'll in-
sist." Zobay had a girl's brown earnest face; above it
was her pale, recently razored pate, the badge of apprenticeship before her initiation into the Komm-
service Martial Arm.

Yeardance got up and walked to the forward door
of the admin quonset, a stilt-mounted foamform
building in the center of the complex. Zobay padded
along behind him. On the porch scaffolding, his
breath making smoke, the kommissar stared down-
valley at the development of "heathuts" clumped together in the village officially known as the Compound. Tonat, the planet's salmon-colored sun,
dazzled his eyes, released them to a matte glare, dazzled them again. Ice trees (in Burgeontide they were
called "blackbuds") twinkled on the slopes, and the
snow—vaguely pinkish now—stretched out before him
like stained linen, as if blood were oozing up sinisterly
from beneath. The Tezcatlipoca Compound, where
the "lepers" lived, was isolated from the Sancorage

buildings just as the grounds of the Reserve were isolated from the light-probe port of Town Tezcatl itself.
Isolated . . .

Yeardance saw the troika clear a mound of ice and
come slipping forward behind three horselike quad-
rupeds. Tonat burned shadows in the snow, and the
shadows kept overlapping one another until the sleigh
rested at the base of the admin building's freshly creosoted steps. The "horses" had oddly segmented bodies,
narrow octopus eyes, and manes like braided plastic
cables. They were only loosely in harness, it seemed,
and the youngest adult passenger in the troika was
reining them in with difficulty. The Tezcatli, Zobay
had informed Yeardance, called the beasts "pequia"
(one was a "pequium"), and they were animals capable of foraging the winter landscape to maintain
themselves; incredibly stupid, they still pulled well in
harness. Yeardance felt profoundly uneasy just looking
at them.

"We visit," the driver said. "You give us heartsease;
we give you welcome."

"Heartsease," Zobay explained, "is an acknowledg-
ment, sir, a general term for any sort of comfort you
might wish to grant—food, clothing, stimulants, de-
pressants, suchlike."

"Food be food," the driver corrected her. "Heartsease be heartsease."

Yeardance examined the supplicants. The driver,
bundled in an ancient colony-service greatcoat, had a
piece of gauze taped over his face where his nose
should have been; the flatness of the gauze suggested
that he no longer had a nose. Consequently, his mouth
was open and his breath came out in smoky balloons.

Behind the driver was a crippled old woman whose
face was distorted by knobby growths, and sitting be-

side her was a middle-aged human being who could have been either a man or a woman—breasts, maybe, under the cassock, and a hint of stubble on otherwise smooth cheeks. This person held in its arms an infant wrapped in a thin, incredibly dirty swaddling cloth.

"Be you the new priest here, 'sar?" asked the driver. "I do see you've come out of Ebarres's church."

"He ain't," the old woman in the troika said. "There ain't been a priest here all the years you was growing up, unless you count Chapanis, I aver, and she was a woman. This one be only a kommissar, like Ebarres, who left us."

"Mayhap he'll grow into a priest," the man said.

"Mayhap, Yurl Stofin."

Yeardance turned to Gaea Zobay for some explanation of what they were talking about; a coil of wire unwound in his intestines.

"Ebarres told us," the girl said, "that long ago the muphormers thought the med-komm administrator a sort of priest, a healer of their mutilations. Ebarres and his predecessors wanted none of that, and—"

"Nor do I," Yeardance said.

"—And now you're only a secular human being again, 'Sar Yeardance, and the Sancorage is a clinic and food-dispensing center instead of a church."

"Good. My humanity is a difficult enough burden."

Zobay looked at him without expression, which was itself a judgment. He'd better say something to these people.

"I'm Lucian Yeardance. Why have you brought that baby out in such weather? Who does it belong to?"

"The babe?" Yurl Stofin said. "The babe be ours."

"And there ain't no other weather to bring it out in now," the old woman said. "Burgeontide be tardy, 'sar, a slugabed green time what should be here soonest, I aver." The growths beside her mouth moved like living tumors when she spoke.

The hermaphrodite's expression remained bland—a face bovine and mindless, the wide silver eyes like windows into an empty attic. Anacephalic? Yeardance wondered. An anacephalic somehow brought to adulthood?

No. Muphormosy wasn't a congenital disease; it was an infectious one, and largely untreatable once contracted. Plastic symbodies injected beforehand *might* prevent the disease; they would not counteract it once it had established itself. Drugs with specificity against one strain of the muphormosy bacilli had no effectiveness against the hundreds of other strains perniciously dormant on Tezcatl. Over a century and a quarter ago, when the planet's colonists had been new to this world, most of these strains had been active, it seemed, and the disease had assumed slashingly epidemic proportions before survivors were rounded up and herded onto the Tezcatlipoca Reserve. The much-hailed prophylactic symbody developed by the galens of Glaktik Komm was as fallible, apparently, as humankind itself, for the muphormers who lived in the Compound had still not been cured. All this Yeardance had learned from the official "book" given him when his punitive duty-assignment had at last come through.

Eyes widening, the sexless creature finally spoke: "We bringed . . . the babe . . . to you, 'sar." A tremulous, halting falsetto. Not an anacephalic if it could speak . . . but probably an idiot.

"Why?" Yeardance wanted to know. "Is it ill?" An odd question, he felt, to ask of "lepers."

"In exchange for heartsease," Yurl Stofin said.

"Aye," the old woman said. "Our god for theobromine, or gum snuff, or a Komm-jerkin, you know, if you got a spare un."

Stofin turned in his driver's seat and snapped the old woman across the throat, hard. The pequia lifted their narrow snouts, dilated their devilish eye openings.

"You won't be getting a Komm-jerkin from him," Stofin said. "You ought to know that from all other such folk you've knobbled at, Radyan Maid. So don't you ask, attend?"

"Aye," the Radyan Maid said, bringing a crippled hand up to her tortoise-flesh throat, "though you do be a whip of winter rheum to strike me so!" And she spat at the driver so that the spittle fell down her lip like yellow lace. Stofin cackled as if *he* were an old woman, and the hermaphrodite drew back, trembling.

Yeardance came angrily down the steps. What did these people want? Why were they behaving like this? "I don't see any reason to strike the woman, Yurl Stofin. If you do it again, I'll have you quarantined up here in the Sancorage. Do you understand?"

The man looked cowed, or he feigned being so.

"Good. Let me see the child, then. We ought to examine it." Yeardance couldn't help wondering why a galen hadn't been assigned to this post. He was a light-probe man, not a doctor.

"Give it me, Dee Dum," Yurl Stofin said, the rictus of his grin suggesting that of his ravaged nose. He lifted the baby out of the idiot's arms—Yeardance saw that "Dee Dum" had only three fingers on each hand—and then climbed out of the troika and approached the steps to present the new kommissar with their "god."

"Have you seen this baby before?" Yeardance asked Gaea Zobay. It could hardly be more than two or three weeks old, though he didn't know much about such things. Its face dappled with cold, it was mewling now. Still, its limbs and digits were perfect. Perfect . . .

"No, sir. We have no record of a pregnancy among the muphormers; we've had none for several years now. Ebarres thought them sterile."

"Ha!" Yurl Stofin said.

"Come in, then," the kommissar said impatiently. To himself he mumbled, "Bringing it here in a dirty rag . . . insanity . . ."

"That be the only sort of rag we have," the Radyan Maid said as Stofin and Dee Dum followed Yeardance up the steps. "And I can't come in for my legs won't let me, you see how I am."

"Quick we'll be," Stofin consoled her.

To Yeardance, under a breath like onions and chocolate horribly blent, he said, "However it be, she can't feel the Chilzentide sting, 'sar; she just can't feel it," and, without the Radyan Maid, they all went into the Sancorage's administrative quonset.

Inside, the solar insets shone fiercely.

Yeardance had to call in Leda DeLoach, one of his five Civi-Korps assistants, from the infirmary quonset to examine the baby. An attractive, long-lipped girl, DeLoach was a physical therapist. On a clinic table in the admin work area, a table surrounded by monitoring equipment, she delicately poked and peered at the infant, a plump and lively boy.

"Healthy," she said at last. "In all ways healthy." She administered a symbody injection, handed the baby to Zobay, excused herself, and returned to the infirmary. Zobay cradled the baby readily enough, but her eyes—startlingly blue—seemed to draw back from the muphormer infant into the impartial mask of her face.

Dee Dum shifted from foot to foot—a sexless creature over two meters tall; hips, breasts, and meaty thighs aquiver beneath some departed orderly's discarded mesh-cloth. Yeardance also noted the fair shadow on the bovine jaw and Dee Dum's grown-together brows knitting and unknitting in bewilderment. Him, her, it . . .

"O heartsease," the hermaphrodite sang quietly. "O heartsease please."

"And you may keep the god," Yurl Stofin said.

"I don't want the god," Yeardance replied. "You've been caring for it very well, and I intend to send it home with you. Along with," patting Dee Dum on the shoulder, "a bit of heartsease for every muphormer in the Compound. Tokens of the good will I hope will grow between us."

He nodded at Zobay.

The shaveskull gave Stofin the baby, donned a snowcoat and cap, and descended the stairs adjacent to the hydraulic cage at the rear of the quonset. She would ask Civ Niemiec in the supply section to procure the heartsease items. Yeardance, meanwhile, escorted his visitors back down the front steps, going behind them, he realized, like a Komm-priest after a New Light mass.

"You didn't come quick," the Radyan Maid said. "I am marvelous half-froze, you see how I am."

"Mercy if you were, knobby woman." Yurl Stofin gave the Radyan Maid the baby, and he and Dee Dum climbed into the troika. The pequia slitted their clam-gray eyes and lifted their long snouts as Stofin drew in the reins on them. They had hides like terrestrial sea otters; graceful, odd-toed feet; and the mo-

bile mouth of ruminants . . . but under one creature's briefly raised, hair-stiff lip the kommissar saw
the dagger of a canine eyetooth. . . .

"The baby god ain't to stay?" the Radyan Maid
asked.

" 'Sar Yeardance likes how we do be worshiping it,"
Stofin responded, "but we'll have heartsease, even so."

On an automatic sled Zobay and a supply man in
thermal coveralls came from between two buildings of
the Sancorage. On the sled was a single box of goods.
Glancing from the autosled to the troika, Yeardance
was surprised to see that the old woman was studying
him out of red-rimmed eyes, muddy pools of entreaty.

"It only be you ought to take him," the Radyan
Maid said. "You do know how to worship him *better*,
'sar." Her tumors jiggled in grotesque despair, and
Yeardance feared she was going to weep accusingly,
melt before his eyes.

But the supply civki Anscom Niemiec dismounted
the sled he was riding with Zobay and carried the
heartease box to the troika. He slid the box across the
driver's seat until Yurl Stofin had a place to put his
elbow—a box of waxy pasteboard, not particularly
large.

"Civ Niemiec, is that all we have to give these people? I promised heartsease for all the muphormers."

The civki turned a bearded face up to his new superior. "The Town Tezcatl Bursary supplies us, 'Sar
Yeardance. If we gave out more than this to those
who visit, *tlachshk!*"—a sympathetic clicking noise—
"we'd have no more for the brace-week remaining until our resupply." He waited for some further order.
Yeardance absently waved him off.

Niemiec said, "Pardon, sir," remounted the autosled,
and traced a new set of runner marks into the crisply

ridged ice of the Sancorage grounds as he returned to the supply warehouse.

"Plenty you've given for just Dee Dum, the Radyan Maid, the babe, Beatl, and me, you see," Stofin said. Yeardance thought this a litany of doggerel.

Gaea Zobay climbed the quonset's steps to the porch.

"Will you visit us tomorrow, our maybe-priest, down in N'hil?" Stofin asked. "—For our *patshatl*, what be two days late now?"

The *patshatl* was a supply run; they were supposed to occur at eight-day intervals, this being the length of a week on Tezcatl.

"Yes, we'll visit you tomorrow," Yeardance said. He was watching the "god" wave its discolored arms and stare up into the Radyan Maid's ruined face.

"What time, can you say?" Stofin asked.

From above, Zobay said, "Ebarres usually had Anscom go in the morning, sir, before the noon-high mess in the refectory."

"That's when I'll come too, I suppose," Yeardance told the passengers of the troika.

With no other farewell to them he turned and joined the furcapped girl on the porch of the quonset—the quonset in which his own sleeping quarters were housed. Home, he supposed. The kommissar didn't feel at home, however; he felt hugely estranged. Just a few minutes past he'd been thinking of Jaeger, the colony world he hadn't seen in thirty-five years. . . .

Yurl Stofin touched his forehead, reined the pequia about, and whipped them into movement. The troika whispered off in a scatter of snow dust and a flashing of ice trees. Squinting against this glare, Lucian Yeardance saw that in the rear seat of the troika Dee Dum was waving at them.

TWO

Muphormosy

Although quick to do his bidding, Zobay didn't talk much, and Yeardance spent most of his day at a microfilm viewer perusing Ebarres's and the previous med-komm administrators' records of the treatment, supply, and rehabilitative programs of the Sancorage complex.

These records—despite the fact that the Tezcatli, with administrative and technological aid from Glaktik Komm, had supported the "muphormosarium" for six generations—were cursory. Some of them must have been destroyed. Ebarres's main notations, for example, had to do with the weekly dispensation of heartsease items and food; his predecessors had been equally concerned with the procurement of the goods necessary to maintain the lives of those billeted under the Long Quarantine. Medical supplies ranked among these items, but not highly . . . not highly at all.

Occasionally, Yeardance discovered, past administrators had dispensed oral sulfones and sulfonamides to their wards, but always as part of a heartsease "grant" rather than as a step in a systematic program of medication. Did this indicate the futility of a kommissar's enterprise? Moreover, the greatest quantities of drugs—still no great amount—seemed to be distrib-

uted immediately after Burgeontide (which on Tezcatl's calendar was the name day for the planet's vernal equinox and, by extension, the designation for the
entire spring season); the Sancorage infirmary also reported, in the days following Burgeontide, a small in-
crease in the number of resident patients—although
releases were rapidly effected with rather ordinary
antibiotics. Very little evidence here, to Yeardance's
mind, of an ongoing war against muphormosy.

Hell, he thought, priorities here are as famously
mucked up as ever they were aboard the *Stella Slipper* or the *Night Mercy*.

"How long were you apprentice with Ebarres?" he
asked Zobay.

At a study console across from him, the girl's oval
head came up and her eyes fixed on him with obedi-
ent steeliness. "A little more than one season, 'Sar
Yeardance. Half of autumn, most of the winter."

When she wasn't running errands for the med-
kommissar, she studied the light-probe micro-codices
supplied her at the beginning of her apprenticeship
and took on the fundamentals of Vencillian calculus/
physics and of slip-fix vectoring through a subcortical
tap-in. In fact, the two chiplike alphodes on Zobay's
pale temples made Yeardance think of the blinders on
certain colony-world dray animals . . . but tiny
blinders, very tiny.

"And Tezcatl's your home, then?"

"Yes, sir. I'm from Town Tezcatl. My father is Dur-
frene Darda, warrant officer in the Komm-service. My
mother is Lisbeth Zobay, adjutant consul of the Martial Arm on Arachne. I was raised in the Ahuítzotl
chapter hall of the Town Tezcatl kommondorms, and
my fellow Ahuítzotli, Niemiec among them, sponsor
me in this my apprenticeship." She gave him this reci-

tation neat, like fine cognac. No real warmth to it, though; no savor.

"Are there any patients in the infirmary now?" he asked her.

"No, 'Sar Yeardance. Unless they came during the night or early this morning."

"Let's go see."

Gaea Darda-Zobay (that would be her full name, unless you chose to add the chapter-hall designation, too) picked the alphodes off her temples—as if they were leeches—and slid them into her study console on a thin glass plate.

To reach the infirmary they had to walk through one of the elevated foamform tunnels connecting the admin section with the other principal units of the Sancorage. Only the supply warehouse lay outside, and well to the rear of, the pillar-mounted complex; it had been positioned so as to make the delivery of goods from Town Tezcatl as effortless as possible. Also back there was a small quartering area and feed-lot for any pequia that might meander in and elect to stay. (Yesterday Ebarres had driven off the last three that had been out there.) The main buildings of the complex, however, included the admin, the dispensary, the infirmary, the refectory, and the dormitory quonsets. The staff consisted of five young "civkis" and the shaveskull girl who was striding with him now to the hospital unit.

Seven people to administer to the needs of nearly two hundred patients. Perhaps, considering the records of past kommissars and the evidence of the maybe-vacant infirmary, seven was too many. . . .

"Gaea—Neo-starb Zobay—did you know that from the top the Sancorage must look like a plastic replica of a streptobacillar microorganism? A bundle of rods twisted together to form a deadly but impossible strain of bacteria?"

"No, sir. I didn't know that." Spoken with a straight face, without even a nibble at the provocative image he'd been taken with. Yeardance felt stupid, pedantic.

"No reason that you should," he said. As they walked, the liver spots on his knuckles mocked his desire to communicate such a fancy to a fourteen-year-old neo-starb.

The infirmary was vacant. Leda DeLoach, Tysanjer, and Vowell must have retired to the refectory or the dormitory. Twenty empty beds, all neatly made with synthafiber sheets, greeted them. Because the solar insets held the temperature comfortably steady, there were no blankets on the beds. The floor was waxily agleam; the bedside monitoring equipment, dust-free; the toilet fixtures were porcelain or chromium bright.

This place is 119 years old, Yeardance thought. Aloud he said, "And which of my orderlies is primarily responsible for the infirmary?"

"Civ Tysanjer, sir."

"Where is he?"

"Off to eat, perhaps; or in the warehouse foyer playing at piece-game with Niemiec and the others."

"Is that what one does to combat boredom here?"

"I'm not often bored, sir, so I can't say."

For a long time, walking among the beds and looking at the metaboscanning heartclocks and the dead sweephands of the aurometers, Yeardance said nothing. Then, at the only window in the unit, he shielded his eyes and gazed out over the snow at the half-hidden muphormer village, the Compound. The stricken ones themselves called it N'hil. White hemispheres clustered in that distant little valley, and, his imagination geared down now to the secret world of pathogenic microbes, Yeardance couldn't help thinking of them as staphylococcic creatures infecting the snow. He shook his head.

"Why is the Sancorage so far from N'hil?"

"Sir?"

"The Compound. Why was the Sancorage built at such a remove from it?"

Zobay's face was again a mask. "The first Tezcatli who fought the affliction feared its contagiousness, sir. Hence, segregation and distance. In those days our colonists thought those the only real defenses."

"But a person who's going to see to those with a contagious disease doesn't do so from a remove. He takes what precautions he can, then goes among the sick and works for them, consequences to himself be damned. If he can't attain that attitude, he doesn't go at all. And since the muphormers are treated here at the Sancorage and bring their affliction to us each time they come, the distance from here to N'hil—pardon me, the *Compound*—is irrelevant. In either case, we're exposed. So why have we tolerated so intolerable an inconvenience?"

"The first Tezcatli wanted distance. So, too, did those afflicted." The girl stopped, then added: "Even in the business of treatment, sir."

There was no need to roust out Tysanjer and the others; nothing was happening now, and nothing programmed for later. Yeardance and Zobay went back to the admin unit—she to her ambiplanar studies, conscious and subconscious; he to the perusal of microcodices of his own. When the girl broke for lunch and joined her civki cohorts in the refectory, he simply nodded, leaned back, and thought.

Muphormosy. A bacteria-caused disease affecting

either the nerves or the tissues, if not both together. Closest terrestrial analogue, Hansen's disease. Leprosy. In fact, the good citizens of Town Tezcatl, ignoring the deliberate neutrality of the coinage "muphormer," used "leper" to describe the disease's victims.

On his single night in the light-probe port before being lifted to the Sancorage, Yeardance had had the impression that while retaining its old and frightening biblical implications, "leper" was also meant to convey an attitude of dismissal and contempt, almost as if it were a racial or ethnic derogation. The Tezcatli Governor General, Darius Entrekin, who had arrived late to meet him and who had seemed distant and abstracted throughout their interview, used the word several times during their talk. Yeardance felt almost as if he had been infected with the disease *prior* to contact with its carriers. But at least Entrekin had greeted him; Ebarres, apparently contaminated by his stay, had departed Tezcatl with no official send-off at all.

To that, Yeardance thought, I can myself look fondly forward. . . .

Muphormosy wasn't leprosy, though. It differed—according to his somewhat less than thorough duty "book"—in its being as virulent in temperate and even arctic climates as in the tropics and subtropics. (For testimony, see the snow around the complex.) Further, the bacillus responsible for the disease didn't much resemble Earth's *Mycobacterium leprae,* and had enough debilitating strains and mutations to keep a conscientious microbiologist occupied at his work forever. Yeardance had already seen the new electron-microscope photographs of the evil little bugs. . . .

What else? Well, muphormosy differed from terrestrial leprosy—in his youth, on Jaeger, he'd never even heard of the disease—in that no incidence of spontaneous remission had ever occurred. Once contracted, it passed through nearly all the heart-rending malignant stages of the most virulent form of Hansen's disease—until death put an end to its progress. Why, this morning he had seen some of its work: the near-total deadening of the Radyan Maid's extremities, the tubercles on her face, the disintegration of Stofin's nose, the shriveled nubs of Dee Dum's fingers.

Dee Dum. Dee Dum. Dee Dum.

Saying this name to himself almost by way of incantation, Yeardance got up and paced. Dee Dum isn't a hermaphrodite, he told himself. Maybe he's a victim of eunuchoidism, a male whose endocrinological functions went awry even before birth. But, damn it, if that were the case, then those at the Sancorage ought to have done something. Substitutional therapy with testosterone might have corrected the congenital imbalance and given Dee Dum a clear definition of his sex. To be in thrall to both muphormosy and eunuchoidism, ah, that was a cross, a terrible cross. . . .

Yeardance walked down the corridor to the dining quonset. He ate lunch with Zobay, Niemiec, Tysanjer, Vowell, DeLoach, and Ambrogiani, the latter of whom operated the galley-wall ovens that gave them their food. Three young men, three young women, civkis from the child-rearing kommondorms in Town Tezcatl, all open-faced and bright and not really much to be blamed for the incongruity between their lives and those of the muphormers Yeardance had seen that morning. These were the only Tezcatli on the planet, after all, who had in any responsible way linked up their lives to the people in the Compound. It was probably a failure of leadership that no more

had been done for the muphormers than was so far
apparent.

Yeardance kept the conversation simple. He asked
each Tezcatli his age, service skills, aspirations. None
was more than twenty, he learned, and as members of
the planet's Komm-associated Civi-Korps all would be
transferred off-planet once their duty assignments at
the Sancorage had been completed. Zobay was the
only one among them apprenticing for the Martial
Arm, but of course she too would leave Tezcatl upon
finishing her term as his aide.

"Won't any of you go back to Town Tezcatl?" he
asked.

The physical therapist DeLoach, a young woman
with a fierce mouth and a quiet demeanor, answered
him: "No, sir. None of us."

"Why is that?"

"Because of the assignment options we've picked,"
Tysanjer, the infirmary orderly, said. He had a blunt,
round face and close-cropped hair that reminded
Yeardance of pequium fur.

"Besides," said Leda DeLoach, smiling, "they don't
much want us back."

A silence around the table. Yeardance knew why
the citizens of Town Tezcatl wouldn't want them
back. So he steered the conversation to the civkis' feelings about the Sancorage—quite carefully, he felt, letting fall no hint of his annoyance with the slipshod
way his predecessors had apparently run things. As
they answered him in turn, he kept seeing Zobay's re-
coiling eyes when she had taken the muphormers' infant "god" into her arms. And when they spoke of the
people in the Compound, he could see that same almost imperceptible recoil in the eyes of the other civ-

kis, too. None of them used the word "leper," but Yeardance could hear in the way they said "muphormer" an echo of Governor Entrekin's open contempt.

Why this intolerance? Because they were Tezcatli, Yeardance decided; they'd been raised with the same prejudices their mentors had grown to adulthood with. That being so, how could he expect anything else of these young people . . . ?

Finally he asked, "Why do you dislike them so? Is it a function of fearing the disease they carry?"

Now he had disturbed them some. The older ones exchanged looks. Zobay, head down, continued to eat, like a child ignoring a quarrel among her guardians.

Thordis Vowell, who was supposed to be his admin assistant but who had spent the morning in the dispensary with DeLoach and Ambrogiani so that he could "get settled," was the first to respond. A florid blond girl with big hands, Vowell spoke so softly that Yeardance thought she must be imparting a first-rate secret.

"They are abased beyond their physical mutilations, 'Sar Yeardance," she said. "The muphormosy has corrupted their very natures."

"It may appear so," Yeardance responded. "Any chronic disease has psychological consequences."

"Oh, this isn't just psychological," the dark, lithe Primo Ambrogiani said cheerily, scratching at his kinkily profuse hair; "it's genetic, we believe—a way the muphormosy has altered their basic nucleic acids and so, you see, their chromosomes. Over the years, if you see how I mean, sir."

Laughable. Yeardance only smiled. "I'm told that the disease is transmitted by bacteria, Civ Ambrogiani; it's an acquired, not a congenital, ailment. I see how you mean, but I think you're wrong."

"However it is," the boy said, undismayed, "the people of the Compound have forgotten—in their genes, in their heritage, who of us knows?—that they are human beings. This is what I argue."

"And since they've forgotten they're human," Vowell said, her voice no longer soft nor conciliatory, but emphatic with conviction, "we've forgotten, too."

"They've forgotten how to love," DeLoach added.

Wrong. Yeardance knew they were wrong. He remembered Yurl Stofin's giving the Radyan Maid an uncalled-for cuff across the throat, yes; but he also recalled the pathetic humanity of that old woman's face before the troika departed, and Dee Dum's mindlessly happy waves as they coasted home.

"This morning," he said, "three of them brought me a baby who was altogether healthy, despite the cold and its inadequate clothing. Healthy on love, I think. They even called it their 'god.' "

Zobay's eyes came up where only her bald pate had been before. "And they wanted to trade it for heartsease. They wanted to *trade* it."

The others looked at Zobay, then at the kommissar. Their looks said, "There you are."

"A pretext," Yeardance said. "Who wouldn't want a healthy newborn infant to have a chance outside the Compound? It's just that the Long Quarantine prohibits such a hope."

Joining the conversation for the first time since Yeardance's initial questions, Niemiec said, "N'hil, as they would have it, is too good for them. 'Sar Yeardance."

Yeardance controlled his anger. "I don't agree, Civ Niemiec."

"Gaea says that you will go to the Compound in the morning, sir, for the *patshatl* run?"

"I will."

"Permit me to drive you. After two visits Ebarres stopped going down there, sir, and for this whole year I have been the one who's been carrying out the Komm-decree of a run."

"Well, Civ Niemiec, you may have to continue going down there, but you won't—from now on—have to go alone; do you attend?"

"Yes, sir." The sandy beard parted for an impromptu smile, and the young man brushed several strands of hair back over his shoulder. "And you can see the muphormers firsthand in their—beg pardon, sir—natural habitat." Somehow there was nothing imprudent or vicious in this remark; it was merely a youthful flippancy. "The runs are chaos, you know."

"Well, I want to go with you, in any case."

The conversation turned to other things, and they were soon finished eating. It was pleasant in the refectory, Yeardance couldn't help observing. One scarcely knew that there was snow on the ground outside, or a colony of "lepers" two kilometers away. . . .

THREE

A Visit to N'hil

Inside their fragile sheaths the ice trees trembled like
dark snakes in cellophane. The sun scowled down
through a biting wind. There was no new snow, just
yesterday's blanket creased and set by the previous
night's freeze.

Niemiec maneuvered the autosled between these
frozen ridges so carelessly that Yeardance, bundled to
the throat, his cap down to his brow, hoped his pad-
ding wouldn't be tested in a spill. The autosled carried boxes of dried rations, a few heartsease items, and
antibiotics for those who wanted them (few did,
Niemiec had assured the new kommissar).

They came into the village on its only thoroughfare—
a lane of ice bisecting the thermotonomous "igloos"
arranged circularly about the Compound's natural
bowl on two separate levels, the second ring of huts
set back about ten meters above the lower one. Yeardance counted. There were twenty "heathuts" on the
lower level, ten on each side of the avenue, and thirty
above these, fifteen on each side. Under the snow
Yeardance could see frozen mud in the heathuts' door-
ways. The entire encampment was primitive—but it
was a primitiveness reeking of the technologically
shoddy.

"The thermotonomous skins on these huts," Anscom Niemiec said, "have a subdermal circuitry which warms the interior, you see, whenever a warm-blooded creature of any sort enters the shelter. It's a Tezcatli system, 'Sar Yeardance, pioneered by one of our early colonists."

Like medieval beggars at a fair, several people straggled into the avenue. Four or five muphormers were coming halfooted down the hillside opposite the slope their autosled had just tobogganed down. The scene reminded Yeardance of a painting by the elder Brueghel.

"To what temperature," he asked, "do these skins heat the buildings?" High on the hillside he saw several pequia foraging the snow—damnably unsettling animals, altogether silent.

"Sixteen degrees Celsius, sir."

"Not overwarm."

"But well above freezing, 'Sar Yeardance, and in the summer the thermal circuitry is neutralized by high external temperatures."

Yeardance did some mental computation. If there were two hundred muphormers, they must live approximately four to a hut. Crowded, but not intolerable. But he didn't see any children in N'hil. The youngest people he saw appeared to be fourteen or fifteen, and one or two of these might not have been "young people" at all—they might have been small, wizened muphormer elders. The ravages of muphormosy made it hard to say. Yeardance didn't understand why the queasy-making rot of advanced gangrene didn't fill the air. Maybe the cold muffled it.

"Off to the right, at this avenue's end," Niemiec said as they cruised to the center of the village, "are the sanitation facilities, sir. They have chemical lava-

tories, and many years ago Glaktik Komm gave them
a vacuum well. They also have a troika, the one you
saw yesterday—it's probably behind the sanitation
houses."

"You think we've done our duty by them, then?"

The civki was bareheaded, his cheeks blistered a
cheerful red. "As I told you, sir," shaking his head in
resigned perplexity, "the Compound is too good for
them—but they think themselves too good for it."

When they stopped in the "plaza" midway along the
Compound's thoroughfare, the muphormers fought toward them from ten different directions, each one
trying to get as close as he could to the autosled. Inar-
ticulate curses flew, and Yeardance saw gnarled walking sticks rear out of the mass of nightmarish heads
and then slash back down. The protests and curses
grew louder. Behind him the kommissar could hear
hands scrabbling at the supply boxes, then could feel
the sled carrier rocking.

Niemiec stood and shouted over the autosled's
windshield: "I'll drive on through! I'll drive on
through and there'll be no *patshatl* until tomorrow!"

But who's listening to you? Yeardance thought. It
was incredible that the civki tolerated this chaos. No
wonder Ebarres had come down here only twice. But
if he had tolerated this behavior, too, it was little wonder that it still went on each week.

Yeardance noted how frail these frantically elbowing people looked, how cadaverous their faces were.
Muphormosy, although capable of triggering nutritive
disturbances too, surely hadn't rendered them so skele-
tal by itself. Divest them of their coats, their leggings, their smelly shawls, and you'd find nothing but
bone. Moreover, there weren't more than sixty or sev-
enty people around the sled. Where were the other

one-hundred-plus muphormers who ought to be here? Were they too weak to contend with such jostling, or were they outside the Compound somewhere? A few, he saw, were straggling down the hillock beyond the village's end. Maybe they'd been foraging.

"*I'm really going to leave you!*" Niemiec shouted. "*I will, I swear!*"

"How?" shouted Yeardance, amused. "Without murdering twenty or more people, I mean?"

Niemiec gave him an abashed stare. "I, murder?" it demanded. And again Yeardance wondered why the civki hadn't done something to improve his system of distributing goods. Was it that he *expected* the muphormers to behave like this, and so let them get away with such rudeness and animality?

From somewhere up the hillside a shrill, undulating howl—an eerie, inhuman sound—signaled the muphormers to order.

Yeardance searched the second level of huts for the source of this cry, and finally saw Yurl Stofin above their autosled, his hands cupped about both his mouth and his open nasal cavity.

"What do you do?" Stofin cried resonantly. "Haven't I told you that coming to us today was the new kommissar, maybe a priest such as there once was? . . . And *you!* . . . and *you!*"—he pointed to stragglers just going into the plaza—"you shame us by arriving late to greet such a personage, first kommissar to grace the avenue of N'hil since Ebarres took sick in his soul seven seasons gone and hid in the Sancoragel Shame to you, late ones!"

The "late ones" were all elderly, emaciated, almost paralytic. The Radyan Maid was nowhere among them, but, then, she probably couldn't walk. No Dee Dum, either.

"Welcome!" Stofin called down. "You bring us heartsease?"

"Mostly the necessities!" Yeardance responded.

"Well, we be good, as you may see! Give your giftings to whoever behaves fitsome, if you would!" Yesterday, a troika driver; today, a generous chieftain. Stofin waved and then retired into one of the second-level heathuts.

"He's a kind of chieftain by primogeniture," Niemiec said, as if he had just read Yeardance's thoughts. "His father and grandfather were chieftains, too, you see."

"Chieftains? Is this a muphormer colony or a fifteenth-century Aztec stronghold?" Oddly the planet's name suggested the latter. . . .

Because the muphormers were now shuffling quietly in ragbound or on flimsily booted feet to the rear of the sled, Niemiec and Yeardance climbed into the carrier section and began unstrapping supply boxes. While at this work, the kommissar saw that all those closest to the sled's tailboard were relatively young and vigorous muphormers who'd taken advantage of their strength to get where they were. Even so, their faces were still atrocities—lips and ears missing, jaw bones exposed, eyes eaten away or swollen shut, cheeks discolored and knobby. And the hands that reached out to receive the supplies they offered. . . .

How do you inure yourself to this? Yeardance wondered. I'm almost fifty and I ought to be inured. . . .

Someone in the crowd cackled. Man, woman, or teenager, who could say? Any of those hideous faces might have harbored such a noise. As the frail muphormers pushed away from the carrier, the older ones made pitiful birdlike pipings while they waited for food. Yeardance was outraged. He could feel himself near tears.

When Niemiec handed the first food packet down to a young woman already crushed against the tailboard, the shoving resumed.

"How many of these to each person, Civ Niemiec?" Yeardance asked. He read the label on one of the packets and found that it claimed to contain the minimum nutritive requirements, at one meal a day, for an eight-day Tezcatli week. Protein sticks, vitamins, candy, powdered theobromine—all wrapped in plastic or edible sheaths.

"One, sir."

"Looky to me!" the young woman at the tailboard cried. "I be first! I must have two!"

"Aye, aye, that's how it must be!" a man shouted. "Tamara's first, she must have two!" A walking stick was waved.

Niemiec gave the woman a second packet, and she squeezed out of the crowd, knocking away the hands of those who grabbed at her. The woman gained the track of the lower level of huts, found a series of crudely cut steps there, and, fighting the ice on them, climbed to the second ring of dwellings.

"Whoever's first must take a packet to Yurl Stofin," Niemiec said.

"But he was well taken care of yesterday."

"These people probably don't know that, sir."

A while later Yeardance saw two men make the perilous climb to Stofin's heathut.

When the kommissar and his civki had emptied the ten large waxboard boxes (eight food packets to a box), twenty or more people still remained in the plaza, either unserved late arrivals or dissemblers who were hoping to wangle a second packet. Finally these people hobbled unprotestingly off. The *patshatl* was at an end. Under his cap and parka, Yeardance was sweating now.

"There wasn't enough, Civ Niemiec. There wasn't enough."

"There's never enough, sir."

"Why? Why do we give them only what will tease them? Anscom"—he used the boy's given name—"Anscom, we're fighting not only muphormosy here, but malnutrition and starvation. Whose doing is this? The Tezcatli administration? Governor Entrekin? Town Tezcatl's bursar of commodities? It looks like a conspiracy to murder by institutionalized neglect, Anscom."

"No, sir. It's not. Town Tezcatl is largely supplied by Glaktik Komm, and the bursary of commodities sends what it can." The boy was hurt.

"I'm going to visit my patients." Nimbly the kommissar leaped down from the autosled and walked briskly to the first level of huts. Niemiec followed.

The Compound was slowly emptying. A few of the muphormers who had received packets were carrying them out of the village, up the hillocksides forming the walls of N'hil's bowl. The people who remained, in most cases, were either terribly old or very nearly incapacitated by their deformities.

"Where are they going, Civ Niemiec?"

"I don't know, sir. They make a drink out of a tuber called brown bottle. Many of them get drunk on it, I think, and roam the woods. Or they may be cutting peat, or lying down in grottos out there." The Tezcatlipoca Reserve was large, after all; its fifteen square kilometers of area were surrounded by an electrified fence with a brede of barbwire at the top.

"Peat? What for? Surely not for fuel—if they have the blessing of their 'thermotonomous' huts."

" 'Sar Yeardance, I'm not well versed in muphormer psychology. No Tezcatli is. They defy our judgment." The boy exhaled an exasperated trail of smoke. "The truth here, though, may be that they don't wish to eat in each other's presence—since those who have, you see, don't want to share with those who have not. It's part of their corrupted humanity, I believe, just as Civ Vowell told you yesterday, sir."

"Share!" Irony began to envelop irony. Niemiec couldn't be this obtuse, surely. Yeardance turned aside in disgust and stooped through the petal-door of the first hut he came to.

The hut's interior warmed rapidly. It had been empty before the Kommissar stepped inside. He looked about and saw nothing but empty space and the ambiguously orange, cantaloupelike skin of the heathut's shell. The skin was somehow semipermeable to light.

They went on to three more huts on the lower level of N'hil's north side, and each hut was empty.

In the fourth hut they found an old woman holding the wrapper of a protein-stick to her mouth with the raw nubs of her hands. Her chin fluttered the tail of this paper each time her tongue swept over it. Eyeless, she became aware of them only after they had watched her for a long stunned moment. Immediately she sucked the wrapper into her mouth and began crab-scooting backward. When she could go no farther, she wailed; threw her head back and wailed. The wrapper in her mouth rattled like a paper tongue. Finally she held up the stumps of her hands and called out repeatedly in a muphormer dialect. All

Yeardance really knew was that the woman was terrified.

"I want to help you!" he shouted against her wailing.

But the woman blathered and screamed, her hands crossed in front of her like the bones on a vial of poison. The wrapper leaf, expelled by her breath, clung to one of her sleeves. She wouldn't be touched.

Laughing, Yurl Stofin ducked into the heathut. "All be well, all be well, Mari-shru!" he shouted, his face alight. The hole where his nose ought to have been was again packed with gauze. "Your granddaughters do not come back to kill you, I truthsomely witness!"

Mari-shru quieted. Her eyeless face tilted back.

"She needs to be treated," Yeardance said.

"No! Happy she is, just as you see her." This idiocy declared, Stofin put a hand on the kommissar's arm and led him out of the hut. "Come, come to my lodging, 'sar. Have you theobromine or tobacco?"

Niemiec, exiting behind them, said, "You've received what was coming to you already, Yurl Stofin. —'Sar Yeardance, I will stay with the autosled." Indignant (as Yeardance felt only he had a right to be), the civki stomped back to the plaza.

"Please come, kommissar. You must see, I beg, the Deeding of our god, dung though we all be."

When they entered Stofin's heathut, the kommissar was confronted by four mature, relatively healthy muphormers in an arrangement reminiscent of a manger scene. Tamara was present, as were two men whose faces bore disfiguring granulomata. A woman no more than twenty was giving the muphormer "god" suck at a slack but apparently serviceable breast. Tamara and the men were kneeling in front of her—not adoringly, Yeardance thought, but in a kind of expectant dread. They looked nervous. His own entrance didn't reassure them particularly, either. The baby's mother frowned at him, and he could see a lesion at the corner of her mouth and two good-sized leproma under her thin jaw.

"Stand, Codwerts!" Stofin ordered. "Stand for this maybe-priest!"

All but the woman with the baby stood. These people, Yeardance learned, were Tamara Codwert and her two brothers, Ino and Meedge, and Stofin explained that after this morning's "Deeding" they would be the baby-god's worshipers until the next *patshatl* run. It would be their duty to keep the mother also, Stofin's skinmate Beatl—who, since she was currently the only muphormer woman to have a baby, now merited the dubious honorific "Womb." On this account, Stofin told him, she must also be given enough of the others' rations to produce enough milk for the god, lest she be tempted to leave it on a rock for the undiscriminating and omnivorous pequia.

Each muphormer "family" would have, in turn, the privilege of nurturing their god and its mother for a Tezcatli week, the cycle of Deedings to run until the child began to eat other sorts of food or else its mother's breasts ran dry. If the latter happened, the "family" responsible for the mother's failure to lactate would forfeit a month's rations to the parents of the god. Or they could suffer a public stoning. Like a Madonna of the Pustule, Womb-Beatl beamed while her skinmate explained.

At last Yeardance said, "Your wife's"—he couldn't bring himself to say "skinmate's"—"pregnancy wasn't reported to us, Yurl Stofin. You could have had the baby at the Sancorage. And if you wish to bring it to

us again, we'll see to it that it has enough to eat, even
without your weekly . . . Deeding."

Womb-Beatl looked ready to put the baby into
Yeardance's arms, but her husband said, "It be the
Codwerts' turn, kommissar. Yesterday you did say no
to us, and now our new Deeding be sealed, I aver."
The gauze over his nasal cavity seemed almost to fi-
brillate.

"Where's the Radyan Maid, Stofin, and the one
called Dee Dum?"

"Down in a below-place hut, maybe—for she can't
walk up here, you know. Or else in the woods, her
baby digging at roots, so I might hazard."

Yeardance learned that the Radyan Maid was
Womb-Beatl's mother as well as Dee Dum's.

"Aye," said Stofin. "She be my marriage-mother,
'sar, and the living nana of our god. We've been rever-
ing her ever since Womb-Beatl's womb began to
swell."

Yes, Yeardance thought, I saw how you "revered"
her with the back of your hand. He asked, "Why
would the two of them go root-hunting in this
weather, Stofin? They'll aggravate the muphormosy."

"Aye, but N'hil after the *patshatl* do be only for the
brave or dying. Mari-shru, as an instance, can't hobble
out no more. And me and these," indicating the others, "we fear nothing because I be the non/ent of the
dung we are and do protect them, you see."

Non/ent. A sardonic title suggesting Yurl Stofin's
preeminence in the muphormer Compound. Because
the title wasn't substanceless—Stofin *could* command
these people, and was doing so.

"Pardon," Stofin emended, his head down. "I do
fear my maybe-priest, I should confess."

"Let me see the baby," Yeardance said. He moved

to the seated mother and took it from her arms.
Womb-Beatl didn't rearrange her fallen shift to cover
her breasts, and from wrinkled belly to disfigured
throat the woman's torso, flaunted, intensified his
sense of having intruded where he wasn't wanted. The
baby, in a blanket only a little less coarse than cheese-
cloth, was content enough. "What do you call him?"
He realized that Womb-Beatl's frown was a means of
concealing her fear of him.

"Teo," she said. "Our god is Teo."

"A person's name he'll have," Yurl Stofin said,
"when his godhood do be cut away. Always till then
our gods be called Teo, you see."

Well, Teo was a perfect name for a god. It partook
of the Old Greek "theos" and exactly reproduced the
ancient Nahuatl word for "god". . . .

"Let us take Womb-Beatl," Meedge Codwert said,
"so's we might be able to worship out our babe Teo
till the next Deeding." He was impatient to be gone,
to take the responsibility of this unasked-for charge
and have done with it.

"Wait," Yeardance said. "Yesterday we found this
baby to be healthy. But the rest of you aren't—you're
stricken with the various muphormosy bacilli and do
nothing to help your bodies fight it. . . . Or else we
at the Sancorage have done nothing. I really don't
know what's going on between our supposedly inter-
dependent communities, even though the Sancorage
ought to be an ally against the disease you struggle
with."

The muphormers stared at him. Their faces were
like New Light equinoctial masks such as his childhood friends had worn each season-turning on Jaeger. . . .

"So far as I can see," he went on, "we haven't been that reliable an ally."

No one agreed with him. No one contradicted him.

"How many muphormers are there, Yurl Stofin?"

"Who can say? Of late the deaths come more. Maybe one hundred sixty, let me so guess." (Ebarres's final computation had been two hundred—a suspiciously round figure, now that Yeardance thought about it, in a report that should have been exact.)

The baby myopically guided a hand toward Yeardance's nose. The kommissar was tempted to take Teo back to the Sancorage with him in spite of Yurl Stofin's refusal.

"All right. This is what I want, Yurl Stofin. I want twenty people a day to come to the Sancorage for examinations and treatment. I want the oldest and the sickest to report first. Have them ready tomorrow morning. Civ Niemiec and another will be here with autosleds to carry them back. We'll continue these examinations until every muphormer has reported. It should take eight days, I suppose, a Tezcatli week. But there's going to be medication and treatment for those who require it—like that woman Mari-shru—and no one returns to the Compound until he's capable of doing so. Do you understand me?"

Stofin cackled. Womb-Beatl frowned. The Codwerts exchanged looks.

"Will you do this?"

"Oh, 'sar, we don't go to the Sancorage no more—inside it, I mean—at least not so the others of us might know about us going, do you see? Except in Burgeontide, perhaps. Since a little time after the first muphormers came here to N'hil it's been forbid. Why, I the non/ent must be the forbidder of it, as my father was." Nervously Stofin grinned.

"Except in Burgeontide or on the sneak," Meedge Codwert said. "And even be you a sneakster who do go up, they don't give you nothing."

"The church that it used to be has died," Tamara added.

"Well, tomorrow you'll have the oldest and the sickest start coming, Non/ent Stofin." Yeardance rocked the baby a bit. "Tell them if they don't come, the new med-komm administrator will order the supply runs halted altogether. You hear me swear it even as I cradle your god."

"Give him to me," Stofin said, not abruptly but in bewilderment.

Yeardance handed the child over. *"Will you do this?"*

"Aye," Stofin said. The others shared his confusion.

"Tomorrow, then." The kommissar left the heathut and began to descend the icy stairs to the plaza.

Suddenly he saw five children on the opposite hillside—all just under ten, he would guess, and already disease-scarred. They were throwing irregular chunks of ice at an old man in tattered leggings who was trying to move from one hut's doorway to another's. The chunks broke around him without much accuracy of impact, and the man didn't even look up. Niemiec, Yeardance saw, was watching this pantomime with utter detachment, his arms folded over the autosled's steering wheel.

Finally a shard of ice struck the old man in the head, staggering him. He lost his footing and pitched sidelong to the snow.

Yeardance shouted something, but one of the children—a girl?—dashed down the hillside, sliding the last few meters, wrenched the victim's snowhood away from him, and then, waving the knit hood in one hand,

scrambled back up the hill to her comrades. Prismatic
reflections in the skins of the ice trees across the way
made the children seem terribly fiendish—and when
the old muphormer got up, one of them lobbed a final
chunk of ice at him. Then the five assailants were
over the hillock and gone.

"Are you all right?" Yeardance shouted.

The old man turned away and stooped into a heathut.

Well, whatever else the incident suggested, it
proved that the Compound did have children in it, or
around it, other than Yurl Stofin's "god." Could it be
that for protection and minor rapine they ran in
packs? Should he assume that the traditional family
units—whether of the biological or the communal
sort—had broken down over the last four or five generations? That's what the evidence seemed to suggest.

And there was more: No children under about fourteen had come to the sled for the *patshatl*. They were
probably excluded from it by a long-standing taboo
deriving from the inadequate supplies brought down
to them from the Sancorage. Since Teo represented
the first birth (or so it appeared) in six or seven
years, Yeardance didn't have to worry about children
under the age of six having to fend for themselves—
there weren't any. But in all, between the ages of six
or fourteen, there must be fifty to sixty children
banded together in hunting groups and raiding par-
ties, staying alive by their wits, their agility, and a
grudging cooperation.

Yeardance recalled that Stofin had told Mari-shru
that her granddaughters had not come back to "kill
her." Is that what one expects from the children here?
he asked himself.

At the autosled Yeardance rebuked Niemiec: "You might have stopped those children in their 'game.'"

The civki activated the autosled and turned it expertly in the circle of N'hil's plaza. "I might have stopped this game," he said, "but it's only one of an ongoing series that we can't halt, 'Sar Yeardance."

"So you ignore it?"

They were already out of the village. "This one wasn't murderous, sir, and the old muphormer, he wasn't hurt, you see."

I'm not attuned to these young people's value systems, Yeardance told himself. Should I be . . . ?

The planet's tiny sun, Tonat, floated over them like a specimen-smeared microscope disk. Neither Niemiec nor the kommissar spoke again, and it didn't take them long to reach the Sancorage.

FOUR

A Winter Evening with
Pequia and Shrunken Heads

Late that afternoon Gaea Zobay and Thordis Vowell
were with him in the admin quonset. Perched on the
concave rim of his desk, he had just informed the two
women of the strenuous eight days ahead of them; the
other four civkis had heard his announcement over the
intercom system. When, he wondered, would their
hostility break and wash over him? Their faces be-
traying nothing, Zobay and Vowell sat mute in adjacent coaster chairs.

"Well," he said, rubbing his hands together, "has
any kommissar ever been murdered by his staff?"

Thordis Vowell smiled. Gaea Zobay didn't.

"Will there be grumbling?" he asked.

"Yes, sir," Vowell said, "for it's not something we've
ever done. We treat them as they come in, in ones and
twos at night, you see."

"Ebarres never brought them in en masse for treatment?"

"He never brought them in at all," the blond girl
said.

"What *did* he do?"

"Nothing," Zobay said. "Waited for reassignment
from Glaktik Komm. Half of autumn, half of winter, I

learned nothing from him but how to affix the alphodes and prepare him the hot theobromine."

"Did any of the six of you know Ebarres's predecessor? Chapanis, I believe his name was."

"Her," Vowell said. "Candace Chapanis, the records say, as does a bit of my memory from the time she was here. But no civkis stay at the Sancorage for more than two years, 'Sar Yeardance, and Ebarres was here for six, you know."

Six years! No wonder Ebarres had been into cacaodope. What had the poor man done to deserve such a punishment? My own change-of-station orders indicate only a two-year assignment. . . .

"How, then," Yeardance asked Vowell, whose hands rested on her knees like scalloped iron lion's paws, "do you have memory of Chapanis?"

"She came often to Town Tezcatl from the Sancorage when I was a child in the Lysander chapter of the kommondorms. Our mentors told us that she made noises in the Governor General's office and the bursary of commodities. She enraged the high-ups, don't you see?"

"To what end?"

"That, after a time, she came no more to Town Tezcatl."

"Because Ebarres replaced her?"

"No, 'Sar Yeardance. She was barred from coming—barred by Governor Mann."

Ah, so Chapanis was imprisoned here by decree as well as by the transparent tactic of a duty assignment. Yeardance was aware of Zobay's implacable blue eyes upon him, but he wondered if he, too, was a prisoner at the Sancorage. Would he be barred from going to Town Tezcatl if Governor Entrekin disapproved of

the way he ran the muphormosarium's affairs? He realized, numbly, that he was afraid. . . .

"Civ Vowell, how long was Chapanis kommissar of
the Sancorage complex?"

"I don't this instant know, sir. I can punch it up for
you on the micro-codex retriever."

"No, that's all right.—What do you think of giving
the muphormers examinations? Gaea, you'll have to
abandon your alphodes and training codices for at
least our daytime hours, and, Civ Vowell, you'll have
to assist DeLoach and Tysanjer in the infirmary or
Ambrogiani in the dispensary."

"Will we be infected too?" Zobay asked.

"If you haven't been yet, I would think not," Yeardance said carefully. "We have the symbody, and I'm
sure, in any case, that only prolonged skin contact
with a muphormer would convey it—at least for us."

"Then the examinations are good, I suppose," Vowell said. "That's what the Sancorage is for, I have
heard."

I have heard! Yeardance looked into Vowell's gray-
brown eyes and found only matter-of-factness there,
the sort he'd already encountered several times over in
young Niemiec. This impassivity was as frightening as
the duration of Ebarres's stay at the Sancorage—it isolated Yeardance.

"Will we cure them?" Zobay asked.

"How can I say we'll cure them if after more than a
century the Sancorage still exists? But suffering—a bit
of suffering—we may be able to ease."

"As we told you yesterday," Vowell said, "they suffer from a corruption that isn't the muphormosy, sir.
Medication won't relieve it."

What had DeLoach said? *They have forgotten how
to love.* Yeardance now had some evidence that there

might be a degree of truth in this, but, on the basis of it alone, you still couldn't declare the muphormers a new and pernicious strain of humanity. Other factors were involved. And these hidden intangibles already ate at Yeardance like a disease whose first symptom is fever.

"Civ Vowell, some of our patients quite clearly suffer from malnutrition as well as muphormosy."

Both Vowell and Zobay looked at him as if to say "So?"

"Improper diet can cause chemical imbalances that affect behavior, can you fathom such a thing? This is in addition to the psychological consequences of a disease that the popular mind regards not simply as muphormosy but as the Red Devourer. Part of it, I'm sure, is that our patients haven't had enough to eat."

"Well, once they cultivated gardens," Zobay said, "in Burgeontide and early Tonattide. *Centli* gardens. But now they care more for only the *patshatl* runs and they beg for heartsease."

"How long ago did they abandon their gardens?"

Zobay shrugged. "I don't remember my mentor's telling me this."

"Oh," said Vowell, "they still make a pretense at growing such gardens, but they don't tend them well, and the bursar refuses to send supplies to make up for the lack they feel as a result of their own great indolence. Of that you must be sure."

"And so now they starve," Yeardance said, "as well as fight the Red Devourer. Meanwhile, the Long Quarantine and the Tezcatlipoca Reserve delimit the area over which they may forage."

The women were unsympathetic. "If they starve," their attitudes said, "it's because of their want of initiative and pride." And the kommissar had to admit

that the muphormers indeed lacked these qualities.
What, after all, could you say in behalf of a chieftain
whose title was non/ent and who frankly called himself and his people dung . . . ?

"I must confess," Yeardance said, trying to recoup a
little of the young women's esteem, "that I have wondered why the muphormers haven't fallen upon a few
of the pequia and butchered them—if they're as hungry as they seem."

Thordis Vowell and the fragile-looking shaveskull
exchanged a perplexed, serious glance, as if each was
seeking the cue for a proper response in the other's
expression. Then both girls began to sputter through
their clamped lips. Squeezing their hands between
their knees, they rocked in their coaster chairs and
then laughed out loud. Yeardance watched them in
low-key amazement. In spite of his utter lack of a *felt*
embarrassment, color flooded to his face and he
laughed too.

"Why is that so funny?" he asked.

"Oh, 'Sar Yeardance," Thordis Vowell said, "pequium meat is like wormwood-treated rubber, in
both consistency and taste. Many times the early colonists tried to make it palatable—an impossibility, you
must see, akin to calculating the square root of infin-
ity." She laughed some more. "If in Town Tezcatl you
are served an inadequate meal in one of the Sciarlin
Street bistros, it's proper to become indignant and say
loudly, 'I do not eat pequium meat!' And immediately
you are either publicly reimbursed or served another
meal."

"That practice sounds as if it might be open to
abuse."

"The Sciarlin Street impresarios, 'Sar Yeardance,
have the right to select at random another customer to

be an unbiased Taster—for confirmation of the offended one's judgment, you see."

"Are the pequia completely inedible, then?"

The girls laughed a little more. Then Zobay declared, "Their flesh cannot be digested." She made a
face that put the kommissar in mind of a ten-year-old
child refusing a hated vegetable. "But *they* can eat
anything. They're the goats of Tezcatl."

Yeardance let the conversation lapse on this note.
He released the two young women from work and settled himself at his desk to do some record-checking.
But each time his hand came up to the colorful shelf
of buttons on the micro-codex retriever, a hesitancy
stayed him. What did he want to know? The number
of kommissars the Sancorage had had, for one thing,
and the average number of years they had served, for
another. But the screen in front of him remained as
bright and empty as the inside of a polished seashell.

Finally he got up and paced among the partitioned
sections of the admin quonset. Console room. Examination alcove. His own lamp-lit berth, with its
cramped work area and water closet (in Komm-slang,
a "debussy"). And, at the rear of the quonset, the
chamber into which the connecting tunnels from the
dispensary and refectory quonsets led. Also back here
was the hydraulic cage that one could ride to ground
level.

Yeardance rode the cage down. He didn't want to
intrude on the civkis' dormitory, and this was something to do. According to Zobay, the civkis had done
their best to prepare for the muphormers' previously
unannounced coming, and he didn't want to disturb
them.

The cage opened.

In the twilight the troughs of snow formed by feet

and autosled runners were shadows on an expanse of frozen milk. The kommissar's eye roved to the feedlot beneath Tumulus, the hill which shielded the Sancorage from Tezcatl's north and west winds. A pair of large spidery shapes moved in the feedlot, and one of them, either scenting or sensing Yeardance, turned its ugly snout toward the open hydraulic cage.

Pequia, of course. Bad dreams disconcertingly ahoof, the parts of their segmented bodies moving as if independent of one another. At this distance, their eyes were pale white spots, as if a pair of coiled anne-lids were sucking out their brains from just below their brow ridges.

That was a pretty thought. "A merry good evening to you," Yeardance said, and he had the cage lift him back into the complex. Just by having confronted those hideous animals, he felt better. Even when he returned to the console room and discovered from the retriever that Chapanis had worked at the Sancorage for seven straight years, the fear didn't grip him as before. He was face to face with it, just as he had been with the mindless pequia next to the supply warehouse. The matter was almost laughable.

Chapanis here for seven years, Ebarres for six, and the average tour of duty is five!

Well, if he behaved himself and was lucky, he still might escape with only the two years that Glaktik Komm had sent him in for. Most likely, however, he'd already set himself a course that Governor Entrekin and the Town Tezcatl bursar of commodities would find disagreeable, for reasons still outside his compass of understanding. Well, so be it. . . .

Before going to bed Yeardance went to the dormi-tory where the young people had their quarters. He knew he shouldn't disturb them, but he wanted human faces. He was in the process of walking in when he remembered his manners and knocked.

"Who is it?" a male voice asked.

Behind the door the other civkis burst out laughing at the absurdity of this question. Looking very much the athlete in a blue night-singlet, Skerry Tysanjer opened the door.

" 'Sar Yeardance, forgive me. Come in."

Yeardance entered, wondering why—really—he had come. Maybe just to place the six young Tezcatli in their own surround. Nosiness, he said to himself, nothing but nosiness . . .

Behind Tysanjer the other civkis were seated at a table in the dormitory's kommonroom. Deeper in, at a study console, Gaea Zobay was siphoning knowledge out of her alphode hookups. Orange light played on her face.

The dormitory was decorated up and down its length with hanging heads, one in front of each berth—as if these young civkis had decapitated several muphormers and then shrunk and dried their heads for macabre ornaments. He stared. So many tiny heads . . .

"They're artificial," Ambrogiani said. "Made of plastic and *centli* cable."

"In some ways it's a primitive thing to do," De-Loach admitted. "But we grew up with these totems in our chapter halls—symbols of the disease we've contained by rigorous segregation and of cruel mutability. Even here, then, we keep them."

Tysanjer pointed Yeardance to a chair, and the kommissar said, "I've come . . . I've come to say that tomorrow will be the worst, I think. The old. The very, very sick. After tomorrow it should go better."

"Until the children start coming," Niemiec laughed.

Zobay approached, stood on the perimeter of light in the kommonroom, and regarded the seated kommissar. The silence began to lengthen uncomfortably.

"Not one of us here is a doctor," Yeardance said. "We have a pharmacist," nodding at Ambrogiani, "an infirmary orderly," nodding at Tysanjer, "and a physical therapist," at last indicating DeLoach, "who may well be here by accident solely, not by administrative plan—since she just happens to be one of those who wish to seek their fortune on other Komm-worlds. And I . . . ? Well, I'm an engineer/astrogator. Or was."

The civkis were still silent.

"No physician for a disease-stricken people, you see. Don't you find that—to understate—neglectful?"

"Ebarres wasn't a doctor either," Tysanjer said, as if this were a defense of the Town Tezcatl administration and Glaktik Komm.

"Nor were Chapanis, Ostiok, Bymer, Siamulunu, or the other five 'med-komm' administrators before them," Yeardance said. "Very strange."

"Well," said Niemiec, "we give them food, we treat their ills, we do what we can. An alphode-fed, five-year-at-it physician would be wasted here, since our muphormers don't come in except for heartsease."

"Maybe. But tomorrow I'm going to call upon all your skills, and for the seven days thereafter. Therefore, even if you privately disapprove the course I've decided to take, I ask your best."

Again, the inevitable silence.

The civkis looked at their folded hands or away into the darkness where the shrunken heads—no, the *artificial* heads—hung. Finally Leda DeLoach halved the silence and, speaking for all, revealed its heart:

"You shall have our best, 'Sar Yeardance."

FIVE

Eight Days

Very early the next morning Vowell and Niemiec drove snow vehicles down to the Compound. The kommissar dismounted from Civ Vowell's autosled and approached a contingent of old people who were surrounding Yurl Stofin on the edge of the village's plaza. They looked like ancient tortoises with sea moss mottled on their flesh.

"Where's the Radyan Maid?"

"Oh, she be with Dee Dum. She won't yet leave him, you see. Besides, she be a healthy old leper, I aver." Stofin used "leper" self-mockingly, the way no outsider could inflect it.

"I want her delivered to the Sancorage."

The muphormer looked keenly pained. "'Sar Yeardance, already here you may see twenty oldsters, people useless to look at, so soon will they die—even if they get no help in their going. Enough for one day."

"Still, I want your marriage-mother, Stofin."

"'Sar Yeardance . . ." the muphormer whined.

"Bring her today, Stofin!"

The kommissar looked at the "oldsters" gathered up beside the plaza. Despite what Stofin had said, none of them looked near death. Of all of them, Mari-shru was worst off—but a close appraisal of the man whose

snowhood had been stolen yesterday suggested that
he might be no more than fifty or fifty-five.

"These are the oldest muphormers?" Yeardance
asked.

"Aye. Much older and they do not scramble well at
the *patshatls*. They have no defense against the chidder swarms, either."

The kommissar stared blankly at the no-nose man.

Civ Niemiec stood and spoke over his autosled's
windshield. "The 'chidder swarms,' sir, are the packs
the children run in."

"Aye," said Stofin. "And Mari-shru she do survive
for her being the aunt of my dead father, and for the
goodness we do her."

Yeardance turned away. Ten to each vehicle, the
muphormers were taken aboard the autosleds, returned to the Sancorage, and lifted into the infirmary
quonset.

Inside, Skerry Tysanjer and Leda DeLoach were
waiting for them with handfuls of sterile tongue-
depressors and a battery of metaboscanners and aurometers. Vowell and Zobay sat themselves down as
scribes, and Yeardance asked the civkis to note each
muphormer's name, age, and apparent physical dis-
abilities—types and numbers of deformities, including
discolorations, ulcerations, scars, and adventitious
growths; paralysis or localized analgesia; missing digits, limbs, or facial features; and the presence or absence of gangrene in any of these wounds. The staff
worked all morning. There were blood tests, urine
samples, muphormolin skin scrapings, haecceitas-
photon graphs, four-color heat pictures for diagnostic
purposes, heartclock readings, nutritional measure-
ments, and aurometer printouts. Yeardance went from
bed to bed talking with the muphormers, or trying to.

They glared through him, or pressed their chins to the green infirmary gowns Ambrogiani had given them. After a while Yeardance just left them alone.

At noon he went back to his desk in the admin quonset. Sitting there, he had an excruciatingly vivid recollection of the face of Captain Michaelis, his superior aboard the *Night Mercy*—the man he had called, to his face, a "surreptitious incompetent." Is that what he himself was, here in the Sancorage?

"Even sitting on my ass," he told himself aloud, "I'm doing more than Ebarres." Despite this reasoning, the ache under his ribs refused to go away. . . .

Outside, someone was stomping on the quonset's steps. The porch shook. When Yeardance opened the door, Yurl Stofin was close enough to embrace.

"My marriage-mother," the non/ent said sullenly, gesturing downward. "From Dee Dum I've brought her and there she be, 'Sar Yeardance."

The Radyan Maid sat in the pequium-drawn troika. Looking through the film on her eyes she whispered, "Heartsease, please." Somehow Yeardance understood that today "heartsease" didn't mean theobromine or morphine candy.

"Alone be my Dee Dum. My Dee Dum alone."

"Let's take her to the infirmary," Yeardance said.

He and Stofin went down the creosoted steps, and for the first time in his life the kommissar rode in a troika, behind animals giving off a smell like oiled metal. At the rear of the infirmary quonset Yeardance dismounted and keyed in the proper cage-opening code.

"A chair we'll need," Stofin said from the troika. "A chair with arms, it must be."

Yeardance rode up, got a vinyl coaster chair, and brought it back down. When he climbed into the troika to help Stofin lift the Radyan Maid clear, he saw at once that under the ragged blanket covering the nubs of her upper thighs, the old woman was virtually legless. But they got her free of the troika and carried her to the chair in the elevator cage. Stofin would not ride up.

"It ain't my time. I do not be ready yet for your maybe-church, 'sar."

"Suit yourself."

The non/ent mounted to his troika, and, before Yeardance could activate the cage door, whipped his pequia out of sight at an eerie stilt-trot. Then the door descended and the cage began to rise.

Disconcerted by the old woman's filmy glance, Yeardance said, "You're the oldest of them all, aren't you, Maid?"

"Aye," she said feebly, "and the most pious among us, so I aver." Then her head dropped back and she crooned, "Dee Dum, Dee Dum, alone be my Dee Dum." The door drew up like a guillotine blade and released them to the infirmary.

The afternoon was a busy one.

Of the first twenty muphormers to come to the Sancorage, they kept back only five: Mari-shru, the Radyan Maid, and three people whose "muphormosy" scars were in fact the blisterlike lesions symptomatic of . . . *advanced pellagra.* Such at least was the mechanically considered opinion of the diagnosticon. These last three people, however, were also missing toes, or fingers, or earlobes—evidence that in the past the Red Devourer had also done its work on them. DeLoach recommended that all five patients be treated with supplements of nicotinic acid or its precursor amino acid tryptophane, and Ambrogiani went to the infirmary to try to fill this odd prescription.

That evening Yeardance sat down in the refectory at a table laid with reed mats and cut-glass goblets. Tysanjer was on duty-shift with the patients, but the other civkis ate with the kommissar. They were too tired to want to talk, but the processed stew, over-heated in the wall-galley ovens, couldn't really hold their attention.

Relish each bite, Yeardance told himself, a mu-phormer may be starving. Aloud he said, "I thought we gave them vitamin supplements in the food pack-ets—to make up for how little real food we distribute."

DeLoach said, "So we do, 'Sar Yeardance, but medi-cation is in as short a supply as provender, and not everyone at the *patshatls* receives a packet. And often if an item isn't a heartsease item, they just discard it."

The kommissar looked at Vowell, then at Gaea Zo-bay. "You see, they have deficiency diseases as well as muphormosy."

"Yes, sir," Vowell said. Zobay remained silent.

"Tell him about the finding he'll shame us with," Niemiec said suddenly. "Tell him what the diagnosti-con and all our tests have proclaimed."

Yeardance had been among his civkis all afternoon. What hadn't they told him? He looked from face to face, fearing their resentment but searching for it nev-ertheless.

"All right," DeLoach said, her voice aggressive. "What we discovered, 'Sar Yeardance, is that not one of those who came to us today has a single one of the many strains of bacilli that may cause muphormosy. The muphormolin tests, in point of fact, were all nega-tive—skin, blood, and urine samples all confirm this diagnosis."

Yeardance took a sip of water.

"That means," DeLoach went on, "that none of them is a muphormer at all, really. They are past victims, somehow cured."

"How? The 'book' on Tezcatl says there've been no spontaneous remissions, no miraculous response to drugs or physical treatment."

"How can I say?" DeLoach answered him. "I don't know."

"It would seem," Ambrogiani said, "that the worm has eaten and moved on. But still its little droppings live in them, these corrupted people, and their genes are affected even yet, you see. This is how it is."

"Not the droppings only," Thordis Vowell said. "They carry the microbes themselves, in a latent state. That's why we have the Long Quarantine and why it must not be abandoned! Their inhumanity quarantines them too!" She spoke with increasing heat.

The kommissar looked at DeLoach. "But you found no bacillar microbes of the muphormosy variety at all?"

"None."

"They are there!" Vowell exclaimed. "Sleeping!" She leaned forward. "It's impossible to seine the body for these organisms and find them all!"

"I've heard," Yeardance said, "that despite the symbody, despite any outward semblance of health, we all tote about sleeping viruses and bacteria. But we're not quarantined, you see. We're not set apart and systematically shunned."

"Except in the Sancorage," Niemiec said glumly.

Ambrogiani laughed, and Zobay permitted a smile to hover around her lips. They were not against him, the kommissar realized; they were against releasing the muphormers to the world at large. That's what they'd been taught all their lives. But against him or not, Vowell was dangerously wrought up and De-Loach's fierce mouth looked ready to take him to task for her friend's discomfort.

"Well, we aren't finished yet, Civ Vowell," Yeardance said, "and it may be you're right. Maybe the mu-phormers can simply grow past their disease, if they live long enough. The younger ones undoubtedly carry the active bacilli, and against them the Long Quarantine is a legitimate measure." He didn't really believe this.

Vowell, however, appeared mollified, and Leda De-Loach's broad shoulders relinquished the tense upward hunch she'd been holding them in. The civkis were soon talking about something else altogether. Envying them their handsome, unblemished faces, Yeardance remained awhile at table.

Later that evening, while Zobay was still on duty, the kommissar went down to the infirmary to see the Radyan Maid. The long room was darkened, and the girl sat in a pool of light transferring the day's notes into the permanent Sancorage files with a telescriber. She seemed to him like a fragile doll (*nenen* was the special Tezcatli word Civ Vowell had called her by once)—but one day she would be a probe-ship captain, and he had never been more than an astrogator . . .

"In which bed is the Radyan Maid, Gaea?"

"The last bed but one on the right, sir."

"Is everything well?"

"Skerry—Civ Tysanjer—said that they would lie down in adjacent beds. They called him names when he would give them nothing but an evening ration and their prescribed medicine. Now, at least, they rest—two beds or more between them—but they don't much like it here, sir."

The kommissar touched her shaven head paternally and stared into the tunneling grayness where the muphormers lay in outstretched silhouette. "Well, we probably won't keep them long. Niemiec says we don't have the goods to feed them for very long."

He walked down the aisle to the Radyan Maid's bed and sat down at its foot, knowing he wouldn't have to be overly cautious about sitting on her legs. Her face, lepromata and all, resolved out of the hospital shadow, and he saw that she was propped up, a tall pillow at her back.

"Come you to shrive me?"

"I'm not a priest of the New Light, Radyan Maid."

Singsong, her voice crooned, "I have sinned, I have sinned."

All right, he thought, tell me what you want to, then. I'm not here to deny you, old woman. "What do you have to confess, Radyan Maid?"

In the darkness the Radyan Maid's eyes were dim little fires. "My sin," she whispered confidentially, "be that I ain't died, kommissar. I ain't died, and I should've, you see."

"Why?"

"I be too old, and terrible useless, and ought by pity to be dead."

"You're not useless to Dee Dum," Yeardance said. "Even now, Radyan Maid, you're worried about his needing you."

"Aye, O aye," she sang softly, weeping. "But Dee Dum he be useless, too, you see, the vilest excrement among us all. And ain't I shamed, 'sar, by being alive only so's to be useful to his like? You see how they shame me?"

As he leaned back, her ruined face seemed to follow him. "Who shames you?" he asked.

"Yurl Stofin. Beatl, my daughter. Even the chidder swarms what let me and my Dee Dum live."

"How? How do they shame you?"

Even though she continued to weep, her voice was exasperated now. "By letting us stink, 'sar, by having us to go on sinning in our stink. I, useless. My Pollo, useless. And kept stinking only for my marriage-son's non/entcy, you must know—him and Beatl doing it only so's to show how stenchful and vile they've the lowliness to be in all N'hil, with their power to shame us, you see."

For a while Yeardance said nothing. They couldn't treat this woman's sickness solely with nicotinic acid, vitamin supplements, 'and more generous *patshatl* runs. Although advanced pellagra could by itself cause mental disturbances, the Radyan Maid was suffering from a state of mind that her society had spun out of itself like a gut-cable. She was a victim of the muphormers' own self-image. And whose depravity was greater here? That of the Tezcatli who had set them apart, or that of the muphormers who accepted their designation as "animals" and raised edifices of self-abasement upon it?

"Is Pollo," Yeardance began, "is Pollo your son Dee Dum?"

"Aye. Born in the maybe-priesthood of Jedderson, he was. You, 'sar, you be the sixteenth kommissar-priest I have lived to see. Before I was god—which lasted but a briefness—only six others there'd been, or so I uncertainly compute." She was staring through him, down the years.

"Do you remember Chapanis? Med-komm administrator Chapanis?"

"Aye, O aye."

"What? What do you remember?"

"Many gods, many gods. Before each Burgeontide we grew perfect in them. After, as it always be, we declined with them. But she . . . she was a priestess of the New Light, I aver, even when her civkis wouldn't let her to come out no more."

"Wouldn't let her out? They confined her to the Sancorage?"

The Radyan Maid began to hum. She crooned a brief song in a cadence and a dialect difficult to penetrate. But Yeardance listened intently and picked out the words:

> O Pollo be Dee Dum
>   And Dee Dum be Pollo.
> All what do cherish him,
>   Love what be fallow.

> Here be the Radyan Maid,
>   Mother to Pollo.
> Ain't she drear afraid
>   Her worship's but hollow?

Looking at him again, the old woman said, "I worship Womb-Beatl's Teo. I do most surely, not neglecting him. But my heresy be Dee Dum—it's been so very very long, I must confess, and I ought by pity be dead."

Yeardance saw that he was not going to get back to the subject of Chapanis. "Radyan Maid, you no longer have the muphormosy," he told her. "Our tests show you don't—there's been a remission."

"Aye, I have the muphormosy. I have it deep."

"It's touched you and gone. It's left its scars and de-formities, yes, but now it's unaccountably departed."

The old woman raised one arm, as if it were a bony club. "A leper still I be! Proud to be so greatly nothing, but 'shamed that I ain't yet died! I have it deep, I do!"

"All right," Yeardance said. "All right. I don't want to take anything from you. Please believe me."

"My guilt. If you be father of this maybe-church, take my guilt off me, as you must needs do for those what's just been shriven." Her hand was now a supplicating claw.

Yeardance took the extended hand in both his own. "Radyan Maid," he said, noting the papery texture of her skin, "your guilt is lifted." At least he could say the words, give what heartsease he could. . . .

The little fires in the Radyan Maid's eyes flared craftily. "No. That don't lift it. That ain't enough."

"What do you want of me?"

"O 'sar, you must help me to die—for only that will lift it."

For a long time Yeardance sat holding the old woman's hand. Then he rose and left the infirmary.

The next day they guided twenty more patients through the infirmary, treating them with a dwindling supply of pharmaceuticals from the dispensary and of food-and-heartsease items from the supply warehouse. They kept back only two patients this time, and only four the following day.

On the third day of the examinations it began to grow warmer, and looking out the infirmary window that morning Yeardance saw the snow beyond the Sancorage decaying into slush. The sheaths on the ice trees slid away, revealing the blackbuds beneath the crystal skins, and the planet's sun no longer looked like a smudged thumbprint on the sky.

Niemiec would have to convert the autosled for over-ground use before the next *patshatl*. The winter was beginning to break up. If the kommissar could influence Yurl Stofin in the matter, maybe the muphormers would soon be able to plant community *centli* gardens all about the Compound. Yeardance realized that the relatively high incidence of advanced pellagra among the muphormers derived in part from a steady diet of just this crop—but with a fairer distribution of vitamins and dehydrated food substances from the Town Tezcatl bursary, it might be possible to lay the specter of malnutrition. Like the advent of spring, this was a hope, a genuine hope. . . .

No one was talking much about it, but the staff's findings over the last three days were unsettling corroborations of the first day's tests: The muphormers of N'hil were not muphormers at all, at least not by any definition confining itself to bacteriological criteria. The scars they bore, the parts they had lost, the masks their faces had become—all were owing to a past incursion of the disease. Or so it appeared.

Tysanjer and DeLoach gave Yeardance the results each evening, Vowell grew sullenly noncommittal, and no one talked very much about the meaning of a quarantine whose principal *raison d'être* lay gutted of its validity.

On the fifth day Yeardance ordered that most of their examination and testing equipment be transferred from the infirmary to the dispensary; he wanted the patients now at the Sancorage to be able to rest undisturbed while his staff examined the young people and children who would be coming in over the last four days of the program. And on the fifth morning a group ranging in age from fourteen to twenty came in as directed.

With them came the Radyan Maid's middle-aged son, Pollo, or Dee Dum, ushered into the dispensary by his oily solicitous marriage-brother, Yurl Stofin. Pollo grinned and patted together the heels of his mutilated hands, like some huge flippered animal trying to patty-cake.

For a while Yeardance watched this; then he greeted Stofin and led the non/ent and Pollo to a curtained alcove away from the milling young people. Here Tysanjer asked Pollo to disrobe—a request that Stofin had to explain to his marriage-brother—and then proceeded to tap the muphormer's chest, test his reflexes, feel about his ribs. Yeardance remained just inside the alcove's curtain while this was going on, and he could see what was also readily apparent to Civ Tysanjer: Pollo *was* a eunuch.

After the examination, Pollo received a hospital gown (his own clothes deserved only burning) and returned to the table in the dispensary where De-Loach was checking the others in.

Yeardance caught Tysanjer's arm before the orderly could leave. "Is Pollo's condition a natural one, Civ Tysanjer? Is it . . . is it what they call 'eunuchoidism'?" The kommissar clung to this word; it offered a vague hope.

"I'm not a doctor. . . ."

"No more than I, but you've had some alphode-training."

Tysanjer rubbed his close-cropped hair. "It's not a failure of testicular development, sir—it's not the pituitary's failure. The penile organ, I would say, appears normal. It's . . ."

"It's not a natural condition," Yeardance finished for him.

"No, sir, it isn't."

"Castrated?"

"Yes. That much is evident even to me. He's a eunuch, but not because of congenital eunuchoidism." The orderly's round face threatened to lengthen into an emotion alien to its contours. "It's just one more proof of what these . . . these *animals* can do to each other! We've seen other evidence of it during these examinations. I'm tired of touching them, sir; I'm sick of the bodies and faces they bring us to peer at!"

"When? When did they do this to him?"

"Long ago. At a time when he was maybe undergoing the sort of breast enlargement some boys experience. Is it important *when* they did it to him?"

"I don't know. But the inconsistencies we've encountered here . . ." The kommissar's voice dovetailed away.

They stared at each other, and Yeardance saw that Tysanjer's eyes were oyster-colored, like a pequium's. He started to touch the boy's shoulder.

At that moment there was a terrible clattering noise beyond the curtain, followed by a chorus of angry voices.

Yeardance whipped the curtain back and found himself in the midst of a melee. Five or six of the muphormer adolescents were flailing at one another, and an instrument cart was overturned on the floor. The Radyan Maid's son, Pollo, lay under the capsized cart in a fetal hunch, his arms over his head. A boy of fifteen or sixteen was trying to pull the cart off Pollo, but to better get *at* him rather than to free him from the wreckage. Pollo was wailing as those not involved in the scuffle laughed uproariously.

Ambrogiani and Tysanjer waded into the brawlers and overcame them with sheer youthful strength, picking up combatants and shoving them aside. Most of the muphormer spectators, Yeardance noted, were nodding their heads deferentially now and backing out of the way.

The kommissar helped Pollo up. A vial of alcohol had spilled but not broken, and Zobay used a towel to wipe down the floor and to pat dry the eunuch's glistening, hairless legs.

"All right," Yeardance demanded. "What's going on here?"

DeLoach pushed a strand of dark, amber hair back from her forehead. "Stofin left his marriage-brother with us, and when he was gone those . . . those *yarbies* there . . . began to beat upon him." She indicated Pollo with a careless flip of her hand. "Yarbies," whatever the word meant, was probably a split-second substitution for "lepers."

"Why did you attack Pollo?" Yeardance asked a boy with wheals and white areas alternating on his face.

No answer.

The kommissar lifted the boy's chin with a thumb and forefinger. "What did you and your friends think you were doing?"

"Dee Dum just be dung like the rest of us," the boy responded without raising his eyes, "but can he dig tubers or catch snow lizards like the chidder swarms do? No. Even so, he do get fed out of the *patshatl,* robbing us at the shoving there."

"I won't have you abusing each other in the Sancorage, by word or by hand," Yeardance said. "Do you so, and I'll discontinue the *patshatl.*"

It was the only threat he had, and it seemed to work. The young muphormers murmured pathetically comic confessions of their "shittiness" and became docile again. The kommissar asked Zobay to escort Pollo to the infirmary and to give him a bed beside his mother's; they could finish his other tests later. Then work resumed, and the results of the fourth day's examinations began, test by completed test, to resemble all their earlier findings. . . .

I've been ignoring the truth for at least six days, Yeardance wrote that night, *because at first I didn't expect such a truth and because later I really didn't want to face it. The Radyan Maid's Pollo is the literal embodiment of this truth, and in his vicious emasculation is a partial answer to how the muphormers have become the sort of people they are. How, though, have my civkis here—human beings no better but certainly no worse than most—ignored this truth, too? Or is it that they've known all along and, knowing, assumed the same knowledge in me? I'm at a loss.*

Then he made a short list:

1. *Pellagra lesions*
2. *Amputation*
3. *Deliberate scarification*

These could account for the mutilations one saw all about him among these people. No. Not quite. What about the granulation tissue in the tubercles and lepromata on many of the muphormers' faces and throats? He thought first of the Radyan Maid. The shadows of his hands on his ruled notebook page were trembling, like huge moths on a metal screen.

Finally he wrote, *Wounded by others, we move to wound ourselves.*

Without willing himself to do so he imagined Gaea

Zobay's body as naked as her pale, shaven head. He silently cursed himself.

Later, in bed, he found another familiar way of talking to himself, and it was a familiar disappointment that the conversation wasn't very interesting. . . .

On the last two days of the examination program Yeardance and his staff had two groups of twenty children in the Sancorage. Constituents of the various "chidder swarms" infesting the areas around the Compound, they were all between the ages of seven and thirteen. None came with parents.

The concept of parenthood didn't have any pragmatic significance among the muphormers—if you excluded the Stofins' fostering of Teo through the doubtful institution of "Deeding" and the Radyan Maid's love for her castrated son. A child beyond weaning was raised by other children; he became part of a swarm, its least senior member, and stayed alive at the courtesy of his fellows by doing unpleasant tasks for them—foraging in winter, picking vermin out of their hair, gathering firewood and drying peat, anything at all. Very small children were apparently forgiven the few hardships they worked on a swarm, for its older members had been graduated from similar lowliness and needed someone to order about as they had once been ordered.

At thirteen or fourteen—later, if their growth came slow—the swarmlings became adults with full shoving rights at the *patshatls* in N'hil. Girls, often smaller or less aggressive than their male age-mates, could succeed at the *patshatls* by promising their bodies in return for heartsease and food. And although the parents of the returning children might remember them as flesh of their flesh, the fact of their return didn't reconstitute the family unit. For the most part, male-female pairings determined "family" in the Compound. Occasionally, as with the three Codwerts, siblings who had belonged to the same chidder swarm retained a sort of brusque affection for one another. Primogeniture was all-important only in the matter of determining the muphormer non/entcy, even if father and son had never spent ten minutes in their lives talking to each other. Parenthood, then, was an anachronism among these people.

All this Yeardance had deduced over the last two days of examinations from talking with the younger children. They were more open than their elders, much given to grinning and gesticulation. They liked to push and be pushed, and thought injuries sustained in falls or fistfights hilariously funny.

In the Sancorage itself, competition between antagonistic chidder swarms—usually five, six, or seven children to a swarm—took the form of tripping, steathily given jabs, shin kicking, and thrown water cups. Threatening to cut off the *patshatl* runs had no force with them because they kept themselves alive by other means—so that Yeardance and his orderlies were constantly breaking up spats and delivering futile, red-faced lectures. All of this was very amusing to the swarmlings.

Maybe I can see, Yeardance told himself, why parenthood is a dead institution among the muphormers . . .

Then he remembered that on Tezcatl the principal means of bringing up a child was the autonomous kommondorm, with paid mentors, its own buildings and uniforms, and a distinctive historical tag: Epaminondas, Ahuítzotl, Joan of Arc, etc., etc. His own staff had come from such backgrounds, and that he himself had been raised by his own parents was, more than anything, an accident of time and place—when Glaktik Komm set down colonists on a new world, as it had done his mother and father on Jaeger, a nuclear family resulted almost as a matter of course, necessarily. Tezcatl, however, had begun to move out of the colonial stage, and the kommondorms were a sign of the planet's maturation.

It struck Yeardance that perhaps the chidder swarms were a corruption—no, an environmental adaptation—of the institution of the kommondorm, just as the muphormers themselves were a mirror held up to . . . well, what? The kommissar didn't have time to pursue this. He played nursemaid and referee, and supervised the examinations of the children.

The notion of parents and children arose again, however, when a couple in their late twenties (who had been examined on the fourth day) returned to the Sancorage with a little girl of six.

When she entered the dispensary the girl was holding the nub of her mother's hand. She halted at the sight of the ten or twelve half-naked swarmlings lined up in front of the metaboscanning unit. Yeardance couldn't help seeing Pollo's stricken face in this little girl's, the eunuch's expression immediately after he'd been attacked and rescued three days ago—except that the child was without blemish and, for all her relative plainness, beautiful.

"Hello," Yeardance said. "Is this your child? Do you bring her for the test?"

"She do be ours," the mother said.

"These are the Gorons," DeLoach said, smiling at the child. "Elata and Bruno Goron, 'Sar Yeardance."

"The girl's name?" he asked the parents.

"Teá," the father said. His body was as thin as a

troika quirt, but his forearms were bottle-shaped and muscular. He wanted out of the Sancorage as soon as this business had been properly taken care of. . . .

"No," Elata Goron said. "Now her name be Teá-bye, and so it will be until Burgeontide and the re-naming."

"Aye," said the husband, looking at his bundled feet, "since the birthing what has come to Yurl Stofin and his skinmate." He lifted his eyes. "But for six turnings of Tonat, no other name but Teá. Perfect for longer, you must know, than any other christling since there did be lepers in N'hil. Now, the Stofins' babe. It do be a hurt, 'sar."

"Less a hurt it would've come to," the mother said, "if we'd let her go when the Deedings ceased. So I aver."

"So you aver," said Bruno Goron. "But now it be to Burgeontide's end that Teá belongs to us, and . . ." He stopped.

Elata dropped to one knee and embraced the girl. For a long moment she held the child in her arms.

Leda DeLoach said, "You can remain with your daughter while we run the tests, if you like."

The mother chose to stay, but Bruno Goron, uneasy in so alien a place, kissed his daughter and left.

Teá-bye, protesting neither by expression nor flinch, submitted to their tongue-depressors, prying hands, and cold machinery. But for an ordinary birthmark on one of her shoulder blades, the girl's body was as without blemish as her face. All their tests indicated that she was perfectly healthy, and during them only one thing broke her composure.

Toward the end of the examination one of the female swarmlings made a violent gesture at Teá-bye—an imaginary slicing from crotch to crown. Then the girl squatted, as if urinating, and made an obscene noise. Teá-bye wept, and DeLoach took her gently into a curtained alcove.

"What will happen to her, 'sar, after Burgeontide?" Elata Goron asked Yeardance.

Yeardance didn't know, nor did he ask the woman the special significance of Burgeontide. Outside, red mud was sloughing where formerly there had been snow, and even the breezes from the north were warm. I don't want to know what Burgeontide means to these people, the kommissar told himself; I really don't think I want to know. . . .

SIX

The Smoking Mirror
Lagoon

On the first morning after the examination program, Anscom Niemiec knocked on the frame partition of the kommissar's sleeping berth while Yeardance was in the adjacent debussy washing his face. The kommissar was wearing only a loin strap and a night-singlet, but he called Niemiec in and dressed in his presence.

"Well, Civ Niemiec," he said, sitting on the edge of his bed and pulling on his tunic, "what is it?"

"I made the *patshatl* run yesterday, sir."

"Good. Is there a difficulty?"

"Sir, we have eight patients in the infirmary still, and for the last three days we've been feeding them with staff supplies. These are gone, and we've exhausted our *patshatl* goods until resupply, too."

"And when is resupply?"

"Another six or seven days, 'Sar Yeardance." He clearly disapproved the pass that Sancorage affairs had come to. He had recently trimmed both his beard and his sandy hair, giving them a symmetry that Yeardance was perhaps supposed to remark upon and think significant.

His tunic on, Yeardance felt less at a disadvantage. "Sit down."

"Sir?"

"Please have a seat while I get my leggings on. It's so early you're starting to list, Civ Niemiec." The civki hesitated, then sat. His face was frank and puzzled now, not the sullenly intent one of a subordinate with a mission. "No supplies, you tell me?"

"Too few, sir."

"Then we're automatically forced to do something, Civ Niemiec, and I now have a ready-made excuse to go to Town Tezcatl. An excuse, you understand, somewhat related to the real reason I want to go there." He stood, arranged his Komm-tunic over his gray elasto-sheath leggings, and sat again.

"You wish to intervene on behalf of the muphormers?" Was Niemiec rebuking him? The lines of red piping on his white coveralls directed the kommissar's eyes up to Niemiec's noncommittal face. The two men stared at each other.

"Do you know why I'm here?" Yeardance asked finally. "Why Glaktik Komm installed me as the kommissar of the muphormosarium?"

"Seniority, I must suppose."

Yeardance laughed. He was holding his boots between his legs, and his laugh echoed in the wells of his boots. "Do you think that's why they sent Ebarres here, Anscom?"

The boy winced at the use of his first name. "No, sir. He—"

"What qualities did Ebarres have?"

"Sir, he was an 0–5 with twenty-seven years' service."

"But what qualities did he have? You've given me a Komm-service dossier description."

Niemiec leaned forward and crossed his legs, an awkward coordination of movements. Yeardance knew that the boy was interested in spite of himself, but that he didn't know how to answer the kommissar's questions.

Yeardance dropped a boot and enumerated Ebarres's "qualities" on the fingers of one hand. "One, impassivity. Two, an ignorance of both medicine and Tezcatli history. Three, unconcern. Four, a profound awareness of his own insignificance. And five," twisting back his thumb, "a disciplinary article six or seven years ago requiring that he be punished for some incompetence. Four of these I'm relatively sure of, Anscom, the fifth I'm guessing at. What do you think?"

"Sir, the man never talked to us as you do. He did what the Sancorage schedule said must be done and stayed in his berth with cups of hot theobromine and his thalamic tap-in to the aeolectic broadcasts from Town Tezcatl. Almost crazy, we all believed him."

"No wonder. It's meant to be crazy-making, this job. And he never went to Town Tezcatl for recreation, did he?"

"No, sir. While I was here he never left the admin quonset, 'Sar Yeardance—until his last afternoon, the day you arrived."

"And if I were to call Governor Entrekin and say I wished to come into the city, he would encourage me to tend to business here until more settled in my position." The kommissar tugged at his bottom lip. "But what if I were to confess we had already run through a brace-week's supplies?"

Niemiec's eyes grew round. "The Governor would be *angry*." He gave this last word an unintentionally funny emphasis. "And Bursar Durane, too."

"No doubt," Yeardance said, laughing again. He looked around. How could a man live in this cubbyhole for six years with only cacao-dope and thalamic stimulus for comfort? "All right, Anscom. Now tell me why you believe I—rather than someone else—was sent to be the Sancorage's kommissar."

The boy wrinkled his forehead and spread his hands wide.

"Very well. I was sent here because Governor Entrekin requested of Glaktik Komm a man who would play with the cards dealt him. Do you understand?"

"Not totally, sir."

Yeardance sighed. He thought about his weakness for toddies and holosensory programs emulating the slip-fix moment of a probe-ship. If only he asked for these things, no doubt Governor Entrekin would be only too glad to supply them. . . .

Yeardance stood up.

"It's very simple, Anscom. I'm supposed to be another Ebarres, don't you see? They want me to put on Ebarres's face."

Later that morning he told the other members of his staff that he was going to Town Tezcatl with Niemiec. Then he joined the supply civki at the garage entrance of the warehouse under Tumulus.

He carried a few toilet items and papers in an effects-bag and wore a lightweight poncho for the journey. Patches of mud were visible in the feedlot, like dark marblings of chocolate in a crumbling cake. Two pequia were lying in one of the marbled spots. Niemiec had apparently thrown some forage out for them that morning. Why do we feed these hideous animals, Yeardance asked himself, while we systematically short-ration the muphormers . . . ?

It was cool inside the round warehouse. The two storage galleries ringing the warehouse's interior were conspicuously empty. If the building were ever stocked full, the Sancorage would have food and heartsease for a year—but it wasn't stocked full. On its concrete floor the kommissar saw only the bulk of two blunt-nosed vehicles, autosleds Niemiec had converted for overground use; they now had plastilax treads looped about the axes through which their powdered runners had been aligned. Niemiec was polishing one of these carriers with a bright yellow chamois.

"Ready to go?" Yeardance asked. His voice echoed.

The chamois in Niemiec's hand looked like a huge shaggy sunflower. "Yes, sir. Did you televid Governor Entrekin?"

"I did not."

The civki made an apologetic noise. He was flustered.

"Had I done that, Governor Entrekin could have told me to stay put, you see. He could have scolded me for my prodigality. To go to Town Tezcatl under those circumstances would be a court-martialable insolence, Anscom, and I *do* wish to go. This way, my showing up at the Kommplex is a breach of etiquette, but not crass disobedience. Do you see?"

"Yes, sir. Clearly." But he still didn't approve.

They mounted the carrier and were soon climbing a hill to the north of the Sancorage. At one point the carrier leaned so far to the downhill side that Yeardance feared he would tumble from the vehicle and roll all the way into distant N'hil—until he himself was nothing but an unformed consciousness inside a ball of mud. But the carrier didn't overturn, and after a time he was noticing the filigrees of moss on the trees and the fleshy pink cotyledons breaking through the soil as far up the hillside as he could see.

Town Tezcatl lay approximately a hundred kilometers from the Sancorage, over terrain not forbiddingly mountainous but still hilly and rocky enough to make the trip an ambitious one. Over a Tezcatl century ago, Komm-service engineers had laid a road through the Espejo de Tonatiuh foothills between the planet's capital and the Tezcatlipoca Reserve—but this road was a primitive one, and since supplies were airlifted to the Sancorage each brace-week by helicraft, vehicles seldom traveled the road and hence didn't keep it comfortably worn down. Ebarres's troika ride to Town Tezcatl twelve days ago had probably given the highway its first traffic in several months, but the thaw had already wiped out any signs of the man's passage.

Yeardance estimated that their carrier couldn't be making more than twenty or twenty-five kilometers per hour; at that speed, it would take them four or five hours to reach the capital. The carrier jolted them over several fallen blackbud limbs as Yeardance made these calculations, and he saw that the branches resembled charred bones, femurs and fibulae. When the carrier's plastilax treads rolled over them, the branches crunched with a startling sharpness.

"Why do you want to leave Tezcatl, Anscom?" Yeardance asked as they cleared the fallen limbs.

The boy's face was momentarily pained. He recovered and said, "I want to leave because there's nothing here, nothing but . . ."

"Nothing but what?"

"The mines. The foundries. Our lagoon. And that which has given Tezcatl its poor fame throughout the worlds of Glaktik Komm."

"And that is?"

Now Niemiec laughed, but as if he had just been cleverly tricked. "Oh, 'Sar Yeardance, already you know, I'm certain."

"Muphormosy?"

"Yes, sir. We are famous, if we are famous at all, for muphormosy—not for our beryllium production or the Smoking Mirror Lagoon. And there's nothing else here to remain for. Nothing."

"Your life, Anscom."

"Sir, my life I can take with me."

"To what?"

"To explorations, sir, such as you have had—somewhere where life isn't pinched between the thumb and forefinger of other men's schedules, do you see how I mean?" This, Yeardance knew, was a hint of the *person* in Niemiec coming out to meet him, the human spark under the prejudices and preconditioning that had shaped his day-to-day face.

Yeardance saw what Anscom meant and was amazed that he had forgotten what it was to feel like that. "I see how you mean. That's why, thirty-five years ago, I left Jaeger, dreaming of glory."

"Yes, sir. You do see, then."

"Dimly." He studied the way Tonat stippled the carpets of moss between the trees with a fragile pink. "Dimly."

Yeardance wanted to say something about the end of all our exploring being to arrive at home with a new knowledge of our origins, but he didn't remember who he would be borrowing from and he feared that he hadn't arrived at home again at all. After the circuitous odyssey of his life he had arrived on Tezcatl, the place this young civki was starting from. It struck him that he envied the boy. . . .

Four hours later their carrier lifted them to the summit of the last hill of the "Mirror of the Sun" range, a hill overlooking the valley in which Town Tezcatl nestled on its crescent-shaped lagoon island.

Twelve days ago, after two shipboard weeks of confinement in his cabin, Yeardance had come down to the probe port from Captain Michaelis's vessel, the *Night Mercy*—but now he felt that he was seeing the city for the first time. Then, he had been dead to everything but the information in his assignment "book," and on the helicraft ride out from Town Tezcatl the following afternoon he had slept. So what he now gazed down on had for him an almost revelatory beauty, like a rose burning unconsumed in a fire.

The city seemed to float in the middle of the Smoking Mirror Lagoon, an immense lake of ceaselessly interthreading grays and silvers, and the lake dominated the whole of the plain beneath them. On the island itself the city's buildings were arrayed with an eye to symmetry found only in metropolises constructed with the aid of computer graphics—but it wasn't an overdone symmetry, because the human architects had laid in cherry orchards, statue courts, lovers' bowers, and even a rollingly landscaped range of mounds for hiking and climbing.

Polarized red glass was the favorite building material, although the New Light temple in the city's central plaza was a flat-topped pyramid built of white marble mined in Surland, a continent in the southern hemisphere.

Three causeways connected Town Tezcatl with the mainland, and at the mouth of each one was a quasi-military checkpoint manned by Komm-service guards. Yeardance noted that all about the island's perimeters pleasure canoes were gliding over the lake, cutting through the wine-colored reflections of the city's government and residential buildings. Silver and red were the colors of the Smoking Mirror Lagoon.

"Four days ago," Niemiec said, "the lake was a plate

of ice, sir. So now they go canoeing in the cold, it's been so long since they could."

Yes, it was cold. Tonat was perched on the opposite wall of the Espejo de Tonatiuh range, and Yeardance's poncho seemed awfully flimsy for the sort of night at hand. Their carrier gripped its way down the final stretch of ill-delineated road.

Tiago Sciarlin, the Komm-service captain who had discovered Tezcatl and who had eventually put down the planet's first colonists, had been a man with an inordinate interest in ancient Mesoamerican culture. His first sight of the lagoon toward which Yeardance and Niemiec were now traveling had put him in mind of the beautiful lake on which the Meshi'ka city of Tenochtitlan had once rested, while the lake's gray and silver waters suggested to him the name of the Aztec deity Tezcatlipoca, or "Smoking Mirror." At first the colonists had called the lake, their a-building capital, and the planet itself Tezcatlipoca, after Captain Sciarlin's eccentric but apt vision. Later this had been abbreviated to Tezcatl and applied exclusively to the planet; the lagoon's name had simply been translated, and the city had acquired the obvious prefix "Town" to distinguish it from the planet as a whole.

The deliberate Aztec motif had become a part of the capital itself. In the construction of Town Tezcatl's causeways, in the placement of the New Light temple, the early colonists had extended Sciarlin's vision into their own lives as a kind of elaborate, intellectual lark. And the similarity of their lagoon to the Meshi'ka one may have occasioned more real parallels between ancient Aztec and contemporary Town Tezcatl existence than they realized. The people boated, gathered "tribute" from the little mining communities dotted about the valley, sponsored the efforts of *centli* farmers on the mainland, and even trawled and cast for part of their diet. The lagoon's waters nourished a variety of "fish," hideously scaled creatures whose only beauty was their edibility, as well as small two-legged amphibians—the natives called them "frogs"—that were sometimes served in Sciarlin Street bistros as a delicacy.

A few citizens, inspired by their collective memory of Sciarlin, adopted the Aztec motif in the decor of their living quarters and maybe even in their own idiosyncratic attire. A number of streets, businesses, and public buildings bore Aztec names, and the planet's sun, Tonat, had taken its name from the sun-god Tonatiuh. Of late, Town Tezcatl's artists—a small and grudgingly sanctioned sect now that the colony was safely beyond the subsistence stage—had taken to depicting the more spectacular peculiarities of the Tenochtitlan aristocracy in their poetry, lyric-mimes, and visual art. With allegorical bravado they depicted scenes of Meshi'ka feather-strutting, cocoa-drinking, and ritual sacrifice. A great deal of this was artificial and stylized, as if the planet's citizens were seeking to impose an identity upon themselves rather than to grow into one naturally; and just what relevance the feather-strutting and the cocoa-drinking had to the affairs of present-day Town Tezcatl no one could authoritatively say; often, not even the artists themselves. The Komm-port wasn't really a frivolous place (only Sciarlin Street was expressly devoted to frivolity), and to many the Mesoamerican "influence" on their lives was a wholly contrived affectation.

Ancient Tenochtitlan and contemporary Town Tezcatl, apart from these contrivances, didn't have much in common. Whereas the Aztec city had lain in an arid semitropical region, the Komm-port was located in a northerly temperate band and went through a metallic panoply of seasonal changes—silver ice, iron and bronze heat waves, golden and rust-colored leaves. . . . And whereas the Meshi'kans had lived with the daily threat of ritual warfare, crop failure, and the anger of their sometimes arbitrary upper classes, Town Tezcatl had the support of the stainless steel weapon of science rather than the obsidian one of superstition. What real comparison could one draw between the two cities, beyond the facile ones having to do with lake life and Tiago Sciarlin's fondness for Aztec names?

Probably none, Yeardance told himself. But Tenochtitlan had fallen to Hernando Cortés, and once, many years ago, the Tezcatl colony had almost yielded to that insidious conquistador, muphormosy. How would Cortés feel knowing that eight hundred years after his death an insignificant bureaucrat on another planet was mentally equating him with a scourge now and again known as the Red Devourer?

Their carrier traveled between barren *centli* fields now and through a curve of widening shadow, but still the tops of the Komm-port's towers gleamed redly and the lake was a mirror of lovely hovering smoke.

"And you wish to leave this, Anscom, when this is your home?"

"I have it to come back to, sir. But it must be left first, I think."

So Niemiec perhaps did plan to return one day. Yeardance wondered what it would be like to go back to Jaeger now—parents dead, friends departed, the whole planet buried under memory's alluvial silt. . . .

At the checkpoint on the causeway a young woman in the violet uniform of the Komm-service's enlisted-grade soldiery came out of the kiosk to halt them. She stood behind the checkpoint arm, the Phaëthon rifle held across her chest.

"Where do you come from? Have you a bill of passage?" She seemed to be trying to remember the formula for an unexpected encounter like this one.

Yeardance gave Niemiec his identity card, a copy of his change-of-station orders, and a signed letter from Governor Entrekin confirming his appointment as the Sancorage's kommissar. The civki passed these to the guard, who examined them and turned her uneasy face toward Yeardance. Through the streaked windshield he could see the confusion she was grappling with.

"You come from the muphormosarium?" she asked.

"That's so," Niemiec said.

"Why do you come? I don't believe you should pass."

"Kommissar Lucian Yeardance and I," the boy began self-importantly, "have come to—"

Yeardance stood up and spoke over the carrier windshield. "Young woman, we don't intend to belabor the ins and outs of our mission with a checkpoint guard. Let us through."

Looking from Niemiec to Yeardance, the guard hesitated.

"Is it that you're concerned for the city's safety?" Yeardance asked. "Because we're from the muphormosarium?"

"I am, sir. Very much concerned."

The kommissar exhaled. "Civ Niemiec is a congenital pan-immunee, young woman, who can contract no disease but the evil one of aging. I'm an off-worlder with a specific resistance to all Tezcatli viruses and bacteria, selected to my post, you see, for just that reason. And this vehicle—this vehicle you see here—just this morning it was nozzled down with a liquid bacteriocide and wiped clean with an antipathogenic, friction-activated abrasive. There's no danger at all. Let us through."

The checkpoint guard stared doubtfully at the carrier.

"It's streaked with *dirt*," Yeardance said, putting as much exasperated impatience into his voice as he could, "not outsized bacilli. Simple dirt. Now, if you will, *let us through.*"

"Yes, sir." The young woman went back to her kiosk and lifted the leverlike bar barricading them from the causeway.

Niemiec mounted to their vehicle again and drove them through. Looking back, Yeardance could see the checkpoint arm falling into place again and the silhouette of the guard limned against the *centli* fields. Then the kommissar faced forward to see smoky water on both sides and the Town Tezcatl skyline fronting them like so many colossal ruby tombstones.

"Sir?" Niemiec said, not looking at Yeardance.

His mind vacant of everything but the colors flooding through him, the kommissar said only, "Mmmm?"

"You lied to that checkpoint guard, sir."

The city grew bigger. Far out on the lagoon Yeardance saw a canoe gliding like a spectral knife. It would have been pleasant to laugh, but he couldn't.

"Anscom—Anscom, I'm tired."

SEVEN

Darius Entrekin

Since the Governor's Kommplex had closed for the day, Niemiec took his superior to the Hall of Ahuítzotl, the chapter of the capital's child-rearing and educational kommondorms in which both he and Gaea Zobay had grown up. The chapter halls were all located in the southeastern part of the city—ten gray buildings, in which red glass and polished timber were about equally predominant, grouped on a lagoon front lawn below a cherry orchard separating the kommondorms from the city proper. Niemiec hadn't yet attained his official majority, and he was still welcome in the Hall of Ahuítzotl, even if he brought a guest.

One of the boy's mentors, Sorcha Corliss, greeted Yeardance in the building's foyer and asked him to remain the night. Corliss, an athletic woman of forty or so, was wearing leotards with a red heart embroidered over her left breast. The heart, the kommissar observed, was not a valentine symbol but a small anatomical rendering.

In the recreation hall behind this woman a great many young people were dueling with staves, fencing, or doing the stage-by-stage dances of "ankle war." But what surprised Yeardance more than anything about

the hall was its floor: it was made of polished hard-
wood, and the reflections of the various duelists gave
them the appearance of leaping and pirouetting on
dark water. The shouts of the young people echoed
harshly in Yeardance's ears.

"But you've come to the city from the muphormosarium," Mentor Corliss said over this noise. "Ought I
to admit you, Anscom?"

The way the boy's face fell suggested a voluntary
part in the hall's betrayal.

"Shall I tell her what I told the checkpoint guard?"
Yeardance asked.

"No, sir!" the boy said curtly.

Mentor Sorcha Corliss, hands on hips, looked from
boy to man and from man to boy as the checkpoint
guard had done. She was determined not to let them
pass if doing so meant to sacrifice her wards to muphormosy. Yeardance decided that she was a handsome woman.

"We're bringing about cures and conferring immunity," he said. "And I'm a man with many years' Komm-
service—I wouldn't introduce two human disease
carriers into a kommondorm, even if the disease they
carried were only a mild catarrh."

"Of course, 'Sar Yeardance, I'm sorry to have so ac-
cused you." She gave a relieved smile and pulled Niemiec's beard. "And this one, I ought to know, wouldn't
expose us to a danger. Would you, Anse-lad?"

Mentor Corliss turned and almost ran from the
foyer into the hall, pausing beyond the door to beckon
them on. Niemiec tried to catch Yeardance with his
eyes, but the kommissar knew what was on the boy's
mind and avoided them. Two lies in one day, kommissar. . . . The civki caught up and looked feeble

deathrays at Yeardance as they strode through the hall.

Sidelong, Yeardance said, "Anscom, only half of what I told her was a lie. Only half."

The boy's stares were deflected, and soon he was lagging well behind his superior. Stave cracked stave, fencing foils whipped through the air, and feet leaped high to kick out at other feet. Niemiec was home for a time. He ought to be happy. Yeardance, glancing back, noted that the boy was dully saluting some of the young people who recognized him as a former Ahuítzotli. Maybe he felt awkward knowing that most of those his own age were already in the beryllium mines or in Civi-Korps work entitling them to separate adult housing. Maybe he really didn't feel at home at all. . . .

That evening Yeardance ate in the hall's refectory, and slept in a second-floor dormitory whose berths reminded him of his staff's arrangements at the Sancorage: artificial shrunken heads hung from the parallel ceiling beams all up and down the length of the room, turning in the last light filtering through the slope-set ruby windows. Despite the heads, he slept well.

The next morning he took no breakfast and told Niemiec he was free to do what he wished with the day.

"Are you really going to the Governor's Kommplex without first notifying him? You may have trouble getting in."

"No, he'll see me, Anscom—if only to dress me down."

Yeardance walked from the kommondorms through the leafless cherry orchard to the clean thoroughfares of the Kommplex buildings. Although you could rent a transport-chair or ride the passenger lift whose T-bar seats endlessly circled one of the Kommplex's terrace levels, the city was made for walking. Yeardance walked.

At the base of the Governor's Kommplex itself, an imposing red building, Yeardance saw several *arcs-boutants* rising from the terrace and buttressing the outward-leaning flanks of the tower's lower half. Each buttress was an escalator tube to a different duty-level, and Yeardance, after searching out the proper tube, rode up to the conference he hoped would take place. A slit-window in the buttress showed him the lagoon and the city below, a magnificent panorama. He began to wonder if he had made a mistake in coming.

He emerged onto a hardwood floor exactly like the one at the Hall of Ahuítzotl. Men and women were conducting business at little islands consisting of a low table and two small divans at right angles. A great deal of space was wasted for the sakes of looks and comfort, it seemed, but the acoustic absorption was good: his bootfalls didn't echo.

But Entrekin surely had an enclosed suite of his own, something set apart. . . .

After walking across the left-hand edge of the hard-wood, Yeardance came to a row of polished timber columns and passed between these into an antechamber containing more divans and fewer people. He turned right. He walked the length of the antechamber. Spokes of red light fell upon him through the bars of the columns. At chamber's end he reached a door made of panes of opaque oiled paper. On the two facing divans here, several people were awaiting audiences with the Governor.

"Give your name and your position," said a man on

the left-hand sofa. "Just speak into the 'codifone' beside the door. If you don't, you'll never get in."

Yeardance did as the Tezcatli had suggested. Since there was no room to sit down, he stood beside the brocade-upholstered divan and looked through the columns behind the opposite sofa. He tried to rehearse what he would say.

Yeardance waited three hours that morning. Whoever left, emerging through one half of the door, announced who was next to go in. Through the open panel he could see only a woolen darkness, but he was never asked into it. The dinner hour found him sitting alone in the antechamber trying to decide if he should just walk in, unbidden. Entrekin, he told himself, probably took great delight in setting up a psychological barrier more formidable than the paper doors to his suite.

The last visitor out at the noon break was a woman who had arrived well after Yeardance himself.

"Did he say Yeardance?" the kommissar asked her.

"No," the woman said, pausing. "He didn't tell me to summon anyone."

"Do you think I ought to go in? You've seen how long I've been here."

"Wait, is my suggestion. You don't want to go in there, citizen, until you've been summoned."

So he sat there through the dinner hour, and afterward new visitors began to arrive. These people were called in ahead of him. Finally there was a long stretch during which he was the only one in the antechamber and still he wasn't called. During the late afternoon he began to feel weak and headachy from not having eaten. Twice he spoke his name, position, and time of arrival into the codifone.

Just about everyone at the conference islands on the

floor beyond the pillars had left, and the red light out
there was souring like old wine. Weary, Yeardance
stood up. Was this the sort of treatment his predecessors had received?

Then his name appeared on the codifone screen:
LUCIAN YEARDANCE. One of the door panels opened
and he went through it. In all, he had spent seven
hours in Governor Entrekin's posh "sitting room."

Immediately he was flash-photographed from three
sides. Directly overhead—how high it was impossible
to gauge—a diamond of amber winked on and began
moving through the dark. He had no choice but to
follow it. It took him forward, turned him to the right,
led him in a line parallel to his first direction of approach—then it faded like a dying coal.

Blind, Yeardance halted. Thirteen days ago Governor Entrekin had met him at the shuttle-port north of
the Smoking Mirror Lagoon. Therefore, the kommissar had no feeling of anticipation as to what the man
looked or sounded like, and in the dark he visualized
Entrekin's pale scholarly face and imagined the mocking lilt in his voice. A man just Yeardance's age, but
considerably better fixed with Glaktik Komm, maybe
even with his own conscience. But the one word
Yeardance kept putting in the Governor's mouth was
"leper," and again his heart misgave him. Such a man
was not going to be receptive to the two requests he
had resolved to make:

—A Komm-sponsored program to introduce the
cured muphormers back into Tezcatli society.

—Additional aid to them while this program ran its
course.

Although Yeardance had spoken lightly about the
Governor dressing him down, now he feared that

eventuality. As a medkomm administrator he was a man of no importance, and this mission, just like his present duty-assignment, was insane. In the end it might well be a matter of whose insanity was the more ferocious. . . .

A musical tone sounded, and a panel slid aside, revealing a square of familiar wine-colored light.

"This way, Yeardance," Entrekin's voice said from somewhere beyond that square. "I think you've had games a-plenty for one day."

Yeardance walked the corridor, stepped through the square, and found himself in a voluminous duty-suite with a red wrap-around window. Entrekin was sitting at a crescent-shaped, modular desk with his back to Yeardance, gazing up at a small monitor in which Yeardance saw his own image.

Then the Governor turned and motioned him to sit. The man's face was sterner-looking than Yeardance remembered it from the shuttle-port, less scholarly. An unbandaged cut of no small length ran down Entrekin's left cheek. Entrekin pushed the touch-key on one of the consoles at his desk.

"This past New Light Day," said his recorded voice, "using live unhooded foils, my partner and I fenced. Driven back by a skillful assault, I lost control of my foil and, reaching to retrieve it, wounded myself on my opponent's blade. Thus, in humility and contrition, do I confess my failings to you." The recorder clicked off.

"That saves a great deal of time," the man himself said.

"Yes, sir. So I would imagine."

Then the Governor said, "I was trying to tell you to go away, you know."

"I didn't know that, sir. But you nearly succeeded—several times I almost left."

"That's the way it will be every time you come here, Yeardance, and I don't want you to come here anymore."

"May I ask why?" As always in such cases, he had begun to tremble.

Entrekin lifted from his desk a "plenipotentiary Komm-mask." Without any preamble he fitted this to his features, leaving the lower half of his face and the tail of his fencing wound visible. Yeardance had seen this done before, most recently by Captain Michaelis of the *Night Mercy*. The fitting of the mask meant that the judgment to issue from the man behind it was a wholly impartial one, a judgment conveyed by the man's sense of office rather than by his own prejudices. In Yeardance's experience, however, the man behind the mask usually began to think himself infallible. . . .

"Yeardance, you're here as med-komm administrator because of"—and here Entrekin began to read a citation from a plastic inset on his desk—"'unbrookable insolence to a light-probe captain of Glaktik Komm and questionable duty performance aboard that captain's vessel. Rather than a full general court-martial and subsequent persona reconstitution, this: a face-saving kommissariat, the principal responsibility of which is your undertaking your own rehabilitation as a Komm-officer.'" It was the mask saying these things, Yeardance understood. Then Entrekin looked up and said, "So I have it from your superiors, 'Sar Yeardance."

"I had no doubt that my presence on Tezcatl was a punishment, sir, but I wasn't told I was supposed to be 'rehabilitating' myself." A slur on the Governor's home world was implicit in this phrasing if he chose to notice. "On the *Night Mercy* I was given a duty-book and told that I was to attend to the needs of the victims of a disease called muphormosy. I didn't understand why a medical man wasn't appointed, but I nevertheless tried to carry out the assignment as outlined in my 'book.'"

"A pariah assigned to pariahs," the mask said. Then: "I was supposed to tell you your duty to reform yourself before you left for the Sancorage, Yeardance. I was supposed to read it to you—as I've just done—as a Komm-pronouncement."

"Why didn't you, sir?"

The man shifted in his chair. The tissue of the Komm-mask could easily have been an exudation of his unconcern, so perfect was its fit. "Yeardance, on the evening I received you at the shuttle-port I had other things on my mind. The Compound and its muphormers are one of the least of my concerns, a business I try to relegate to those who know what's going on out there and who care a little about it. I *don't* care about it, Yeardance; I don't have *time* to care about it. My assumption was that once you got out there you'd learn from Ebarres the extent and the meaning of your responsibilities. At any rate, that was my assumption once I realized that I hadn't read the official citation probe-communicated to me from Glaktik Komm before your arrival. That afternoon my mind was elsewhere. We'd spent the morning discussing beryllium export, Yeardance, and more discussions were to follow the next day."

Because Entrekin was now speaking as himself, the mask ought to have come off. It remained, however—a skin interposed between the man and his confession. Yeardance nevertheless believed the confession; for

Governor Entrekin this whole matter was an annoying
trifle, nothing more. Hence, his long wait in the antechamber. He was lucky to have got in at all.

"Did Ebarres rehabilitate himself, sir?"

"I never met Ebarres. Vice-Governor Udnas saw the
man off."

"He was here *six* years, sir."

"And I have been in my present position only two.
Moreover, Yeardance, it's my understanding that Sancorage kommissars aren't to have free access to Town
Tezcatl. They're to stay put until they're adjudged fit
to return to probe-fleet Komm-service."

"Adjudged fit by whom, sir? Who makes such a
judgment if I must never leave the Sancorage?"

The Governor got up and walked across his duty-
suite, pausing at the wrap-around window. Beside
him was a glass bell taller than he was—Yeardance
had taken it for a terrarium, since in addition to some
tracer ferns it contained a treelike plant boasting a
good many pinkish-white blossoms. Then the kommissar was sure that he saw the inner petals of some of
these flowers vibrating intensely. The Governor, his
hands at his back, peered into the bell.

"Reports are filed," he said simply. Before Yeardance could review the implications of this comment,
he asked, "Have you ever seen a hummingbird, kommissar? A terrestrial hummingbird?"

"No, sir."

Entrekin motioned Yeardance over. At the glass bell
he peered in to see three or four tiny, gem-bright
birds hovering at the lips of flowers. Darting from
blossom to blossom, they seemed to move in teleporta-
tional bursts. Yeardance thought inevitably of light-
probing. . . .

"They have a feeder in there," Entrekin said, "but

the flowers—even sucked dry—are a greater attraction."

At sunset a mist lay upon the western expanse of the lagoon; the mirror was "smoking."

"Sir," Yeardance said, "may I tell you what I've discovered while acting as the Sancorage's kommissar rather than trying to reform myself?"

The mask was abstracted, aloof. "All right."

"The muphormers aren't muphormers at all, sir."

Entrekin turned to face him, but the mask gave no indication of his feelings and his mouth didn't move.

"Not a one of them in the Compound has the disease, sir. Once perhaps, but no longer. Their deformities, their mutilations—"

"Yeardance, I don't want to know what those people do to themselves out there, do you understand?"

"Yes, sir." Did the Governor, too, believe them genetically warped away from the virtues of civilization?

"When I took this office two years ago, kommissar, I believe I received a memo to the effect that the disease had been eradicated—eradicated some time ago, in fact. As a muphormosarium the Sancorage is a wholly obsolete institution." The Governor said this offhandedly, as if it had no significance at all.

Yeardance stared at his superior. "Why, then, the Long Quarantine? Why the pretense of a 'med-komm administrator' and a Sancorage? These people ought to be reintegrated into Tezcatli society."

"Oh, I agree. At least with the notion of making them once again useful to the principal endeavors of our colony—*if* that were possible."

In the glass bell a hummingbird disappeared from one blossom's mouth, popped into existence at another. Where had it been in the interval? It seemed to

Yeardance that a nullity of the same sort separated him from the Governor; they couldn't demonstrate to each other the continuousness of what they were talking about.

"Then why *haven't* they been reintegrated, sir? Surely you don't believe them corrupt in their essential humanity?"

"I'm afraid I may, kommissar. But that isn't to the point."

"What is, then?"

Entrekin's mouth turned down at one corner as if he were sucking on a tooth. "The muphormers, Yeardance, don't *want* to return to Town Tezcatl—they're happy where they are."

Yeardance said nothing.

"You don't believe me? Do you fail to understand, too, that the 'Long Quarantine' is an officially sanctioned myth whose purpose is to keep our people away from the grounds we've deeded to the muphormers?"

"Sir—" Yeardance looked across the island at Tonat's last rays glinting off the lagoon. "You're telling me your citizens believe muphormosy's still a threat to them even though you, their Governor, realize it isn't?"

"That's what I'm telling you, Yeardance."

"And that it's benevolence that keeps the 'Long Quarantine' in effect, a benevolence toward the muphormers?"

"Aye, if you like. Athough I'll admit here, Yeardance, that our 'benevolence' is an intellectual and moral one quite divorced from our feelings about the muphormers themselves. They disgust us, but we recognize their right to life and so honor the deeding of their reservation to them and attempt to protect them from those independent-minded Tezcatli who would move into the area to build communities there. When the snow's completely gone, and the mud too, you'll see that it's quite an attractive bit of land, Yeardance. It really is." The Governor's use of "we" and "our" was again clearly in the spirit of the Komm-mask, but he continued to mix the administrative with the personal.

"Right now, at this stage in our colony's development," he went on, "our government and our population must be strongly concentrated. Centralized. We don't encourage the proliferation of separate communities, Yeardance—except for those that grow up naturally around our mining operations. So the myth of the Long Quarantine redounds to the benefit of both our colony and the muphormers, who don't wish to be a contributing part of it. The fear of muphormosy, you see, is a two-edged weapon."

All right. He saw. Governor Entrekin was going to have no part of his proposal to reintroduce the muphormers into the colony's life, essentially on the grounds that they *liked* the status quo. To challenge the man on the issue would be to call him a liar, unless Yeardance could convince Entrekin that he was in possession of only a scant handful of the facts. And Yeardance didn't feel up to the effort.

Outside, the sky bled its way to full twilight.

"Sir," Yeardance said finally, "I will, as you suggest, attempt to use my kommissariat to reform myself, but—"

"Fine. Because that's what it's for. That's almost solely what it's for, and if you don't rehabilitate, your career's over, Yeardance."

"Yes, sir. But I'd still like to make a request on behalf of the 'muphormers' whom I ostensibly represent. May I?"

"Go ahead."

"The weekly *patshatl* runs that we make to the Compound—"

"They remain a part of your duty there, Yeardance. But you can delegate them if you like—that's what Ebarres did, I understand."

"Yes, sir. But these runs—the goods we distribute— are insufficient to meet the needs of the people out there. We're always short. Many of our wards are suffering from deficiency diseases, sir. Malnutrition. Whereas muphormosy isn't a concern at all, anymore."

"Is that right?" Entrekin's voice conveyed surprise, not indifference.

"Yes, sir."

"Yeardance, I don't know anything at all about that. And I'm ready to go home. What is it you want? An assurance of more supplies?"

"That would be a start, sir."

The Governor took his arm and turned Yeardance brusquely toward him. "Kommissar, I don't want to be spoken to of 'starts,' do you hear me? The word suggests you have some further demand on my time, and you don't."

Entrekin released his arm. "However," he said suddenly, "I'm going to refer you to our bursar of commodities, Thérèse Durane, and ask you to apply to her for any further assistance in the way of goods. And if she can't provide you with these, she may be able to give you an explanation instead. I can't. The matter of supplying the Sancorage is one I've never had anything to do with, Yeardance, and I don't intend to involve myself with it now. Beyond this referral, you understand."

"Yes, sir. I appreciate the referral."

"Fine. Where are you staying?"

Yeardance told him.

"This evening, then, you'll receive a televid call from Bursar Durane. I suggest you outline the problem for her. In the morning, though, I want you to go back to the Sancorage and *stay* there until you're given leave to do otherwise."

How long would that be? Yeardance wondered. Two years? Six? "As you direct, sir," he said aloud.

"Good. Another thing I direct you, Yeardance, is to say nothing to Bursar Durane, or anyone else you encounter in Town Tezcatl, about the muphormers' being 'cured.' You and I, and my predecessors in this office, are the sole repositories of that knowledge on Tezcatl; I want it to remain that way."

"My staff knows, sir. And the muphormers themselves."

"Well, your quarantined lepers won't let the truth out, Yeardance, and the civkis working with you will be transferred off planet once their duty-assignments at the Sancorage have run their course. Who came with you?"

"Civ Anscom Niemiec." *My quarantined lepers . . .*

"All right. Tell him what I've told you. And rectify any damage you've inflicted on the myth since your arrival. Do these things, Yeardance."

Yeardance resented saying the inevitable "Yes, sir."

Then Governor Entrekin, still masked, bid the kommissar goodbye, as if his presence had subtly contaminated the room. But before Yeardance could exit, the Governor said, "Do you know what would really be the best for all of us? I mean, clearly the best?"

"No, sir."

"If your lepers were simply to die off, as they seem to wish to do." Entrekin took off the Komm-mask and held it loosely in one hand, like a helmet one removes after combat. "And I don't mean that cruelly, Year-dance; I mean that to embody the only realistic solution to both their dilemma and ours, you see. Realistic in terms of what we can do and what they'll permit us to do. Do you see?"

"I don't know, sir."

"Of course," the Governor concluded, seemingly with no irony at all, "if they were all to die, men like you would have to go elsewhere to save face for your petty impertinences." His expression betrayed puzzlement. Two fingers through its eye-holes, the mask dangled from his hand.

Later Yeardance was to write in his journal of confessions, *My exit was a confused one. I went back through the darkness I had entered by, knowing that the Governor must have a private exit of his own— maybe a shinny pole through his terrarium to street level. I could imagine hummingbirds drilling at his ears as he slid down it to the street.*

In the stupor that came upon me later, after my visit to Sciarlin Street with Bursar Durane, one of my recurring images was this: The Governor bid me farewell holding his mask in one hand, but his own features were made of tissue paper lacquered to a high gloss while the mask dangling from his fingers was made of flesh. . . .

Only fifteen minutes after arriving back at the Hall of Ahuítzotl, Yeardance was called away from his first meal of the day for a televid communication. He excused himself from Mentor Corliss and Civ Niemiec and followed a six-year-old Ahuítzotli down a flight of wooden stairs into a carpeted room where televid consoles were arranged in booths around the walls.

His guide—a little girl who reminded him of Teá-bye, by not in the least resembling her—showed him to the proper one.

The face confronting him belonged to a woman—a handsomely bony face with tightly curled hair and darkly olive skin. Thirty-eight to forty-three, Yeardance estimated, Earth standard.

The little girl at his elbow leaned over the screen to punch the key that would turn him into a face for the woman staring up from the screen. Then the child left. Interference lines buckled across the televid image, after which the woman's face reformed.

"Lucian Yeardance?"

Knowing that she was no longer blind. Yeardance only nodded.

"I'm Thérèse Durane, bursar of commodities. Governor Entrekin asked me to contact you about the matter of supplying the Sancorage."

Yeardance could tell the woman was evaluating him, maybe even for his physical attractiveness. Fair enough. Automatically, without much interest, he had already evaluated *her* and found her . . . what? . . . well, handsome, he had to suppose. The rating was more a product of his eyes than his libido. Bursar Durane had a handsome face whose angularity saved it from being superficially exotic.

"Have I interrupted anything of importance?" she asked. He was making her uneasy with his silence.

"Only my dinner," he said at last.

"Which I haven't had yet. Must you go back to the meal you've begun, 'Sar Yeardance, or would you join me on Sciarlin Street for a meal? There we could discuss—at our ease, I think—the matter you have on your mind."

"All right." A dinner invitation. Yeardance understood that she would probably not have invited him if she had discovered an unsavoriness in him, a repellent feature or twitch. Very good. A sop for his ego . . .

"Fine, 'Sar Yeardance. Is it possible for you to meet me at the Xipe Totec bistro in thirty or forty minutes? Later than that, I think, and we would both grow frail and faint. From the deprivation."

"Yes, it's possible. I'll have someone show me the way."

"Very good." She smiled. Interference lines buckled across her smile and she was gone.

The kommissar sat over her faded image for a moment. Then he got up and climbed the stairs to the refectory.

EIGHT

At the Xipe Totec

Niemiec took him to Sciarlin Street. They traveled by chairlift, in a capsule made of carven purplish wood and smoked glass. The Street of the Bistros lay on the northeastern flank of the island, and they had nearly an entire city to cross: a corner of the Kommplex, residential towers, parks, the New Light temple, solar stations, Komm-service billets, refineries, and processing plants. They passed all these at a cruising level only a meter or so above a grown man's head, for the architecture of Town Tezcatl was such that an open corridor always lay before them through both buildings and trees.

Now, riding beside Niemiec, Yeardance thought of the Governor's response to his question about who judges the performance of a med-komm administrator: "Reports are filed," the man had said. Well, who filed the reports? No one in the Governor's Kommplex could possibly sit in judgment of him without reports, and no one could provide these but . . . the members of his own staff. Had Ebarres's staff had something to do with that man's remaining at the Sancorage for six years? Yeardance didn't want to dwell on the possibility. . . .

"The Xipe Totec's an interesting place," Anscom

was saying. "Nightly they have mime dramas by sanctioned artists. You'll probably see one."

"Well, I'd better enjoy it. Entrekin says I won't be
coming back to Town Tezcatl very soon."

The boy, not knowing how to respond, grimaced
sympathetically.

Except for the lights behind its facades of glass,
thermoplastic, and attenuated polymer, the city was
dark now. The kommissar occasionally had a glimpse
of the lagoon and all the ruby frequencies playing
upon its waters.

On Jaeger there had been nothing to match this—
only way-ranches on the desert and specimen silos on
the barren coasts. Wait, Yeardance told himself. Put
Jaeger out of your mind. If you don't, you'll drown in
a futile evocation. Concentrate on the pragmatic reality of your interview with Bursar Durane. . . .

Sciarlin Street was aswirl with people and pennants
and even window glass in which deliquescent yellows
and blues seemed to float, marbling the interiors of
dining and entertainment establishments with wheel-
ing galaxy arms and mutating shadow-eels.

Yeardance and Niemiec fell into this color from
their capsule, stepping to the disembarkation platform
at the head of Sciarlin Street. The rubies and pearl-
grays of the city proper had been washed back as if
by a tide of fluorescent diatoms. For no good reason,
Yeardance felt like a man thrown from a dull drugged
sleep into a nightmare. The lights weren't that agoniz-
ingly bright, after all, and the people strolling from
bistrofront to the doors of hologravure houses were
ordinary enough in their appearance. You could find
evidence of the street's connection to day-to-day reality just by looking down: hairline fissures in the walk,

discarded placenol vials, stains that could be either alcohol or vomit. Even here.

"The Xipe Totec's midway along, sir. Come with me."

He followed the boy to the bistrofront, a marbled window which returned their images pied with running light.

Protected by a gate of bamboolike poles, the "foyer" of the Xipe Totec could be entered only when the gate clacked back on itself to reveal the waiting elevator cage. The bistro's real entrance was on the second landing, and everything below it constituted the establishment's "well"—kitchens, privacy berths, debussies. An *orkhēstra* apron extended out beneath the tiers of diners so that they might comfortably watch the mimes presented in the well. The floor of each tier was made of conifer timber, and you could smell a preservative resin all through the Xipe Totec.

"Do you want me to come back for you, 'Sar Yeardance?"

"Does the lift run all night?"

"Yes, sir."

"Then I think I can find my way home well enough, Anscom." *Home* . . .

The boy bid him goodbye and Yeardance rode the cage to the second landing. The incense of resin filled his nostrils. He felt disoriented. With three or four other people he peered down from the landing rail into the darkened semicircle of the *orkhēstra*. He heard the pad of bare feet down there and perhaps saw the shadow of a performer. He heard, too, the twang of a primitive instrument.

"They're preparing for the mime," a woman said.

Wooden stairs came down to the landing at each of its ends, and soon the major domo of the Xipe Totec, a graying man in a shirt and trousers of white cotton, descended the left-hand set of stairs and led the party ahead of the kommissar up the opposite one. In four or five minutes he returned, asked Yeardance his name, and then led him to the bursar's table.

Thérèse Durane rose to take Yeardance's hand. Her table was three tiers above the second-floor landing, and the kommissar feared that his weakness, hunger, and vertigo would send him spiraling into the well. He touched the woman's hand and clumsily sat down.

"Forgive me." He put one hand on the polished railing and looked up repentantly.

The bursar sat down. "Entrekin made you wait all day in his antechamber and you didn't eat."

"I waited," Yeardance confirmed. "And I didn't eat."

"Then I did interrupt something of importance. If only you're strong enough to lift a fork, it's no matter, kommissar—I've already placed our orders."

"Good."

She wore white, a garment like an abbreviated sari, her head wrapped in a fold of its whiteness. She studied Yeardance with an interest different from that she'd shown during her call. She's wondering, he told himself, if she hasn't made a mistake in committing herself to dinner with so minor an official. She was looking at his hands.

"I'm forty-nine," he said suddenly. "I think. After your thousandth slip-fix it's difficult to keep track."

"By an odd coincidence of contrivance I'm almost forty-nine too—though that's by Tezcatli years rather than standard ones. I don't feel particularly old, however. I've always felt like a civki fresh from his chapter hall."

"To which one did you belong?"

"The Hall of Lysander."

Yeardance said that he had a staff member or two from that hall, but he couldn't remember which ones. He threw out his civkis' names for the bursar. Then he silently castigated himself because this manner of establishing rapport reminded him of his youth on Jaeger and his friends there, all their names forgotten. "Have you met the operator of the K-line way-ranch?" somebody would ask. "Do you know Civ Townlee from the Gortier Dunes?" The kommissar had trouble, now, imagining Bursar Durane growing up in one of Town Tezcatl's kommondorms. She was further removed from that time than she realized, he felt. Their common denominator wasn't people, anyway—it was the supplying of the muphormers in the Compound.

"No," Thérèse Durane said, "I don't know any of those people, but it's been . . . how many years . . . ?"

Their meals came—up from the kitchens through a dumbwaiter column, carved in totemic fashion, set back from the outer edge of the tier. A man and a woman dressed in white cottons did the serving. The bursar and the kommissar were provided with silverware and ivory chopsticks, root tea and theobromine, and vitamin units with syringes of citrus extract. The main course consisted of braised coney, stuffed lagoon crab, *centli* cakes under a dark meat sauce, and eggcups containing tiny vegetable casseroles. Bursar Durane picked up her chopsticks.

"Do you wish alcohol?" she asked him.

"Rum," he said, "or a facsimile." —And the male Totecan brought him a synthetic specter of the real thing. He sipped at it appreciatively, savoring its burn.

As they ate, Thérèse Durane talked. She combined the two activities skillfully, and Yeardance admired

her self-possession. In fact, he found himself paying
almost as much attention to her agility in balancing
eating against talking as he did to what she said. Although she never spoke around her food, her speech
seemed a continuous phenomenon, like music or running water. Somehow, though, she was managing—
between words, or sentences, or paragraphs—to make
neat excavations in her casserole and entrées. Food
disappeared as if into an invisible friend at her elbow.
No mean feat, such graceful legerdemain, and Yeardance began to like the bursar—surely this talent hinted
at other, even more admirable qualities in her
makeup. Compassion, for instance.

Or perhaps not . . .

"Governor Entrekin tells me you don't believe the
muphormers are being adequately supplied."

Yeardance nodded.

"The Sancorage," Bursar Durane admitted, "is one
of the very least of our priorities in the distribution of
foodstuffs." The institutions taking precedence were
the kommondorms, local medical facilities, outlying
beryllium extraction companies, the communal messes
of the refineries and processing plants, the refectories
of the residential towers, etc., etc. One of the priority
institutions was amusement centers, such as the Xipe
Totec. The Sancorage, since it played an "auxiliary or
nonsupportive role" in the existence of the colony, was
near the bottom of the list.

"Another difficulty, 'Sar Yeardance, is that we have
two sources of supply ourselves—light-probe vessels of
the Komm-fleet and our own agrarian, fishing, and
hunting industries. Ideally, everything that is distrib-
uted is supposed to come through the clearinghouse of
my office. The fact is, kommissar, only those goods
arriving as imports from Komm-fleet are closely

enough monitored to insure their reaching—in their entirety, you understand—our 'disbursement stations.' Locally produced raw goods, now that our colony has survived its infancy, are more difficult to control. Each Tezcatli licensed as an agrarianist must make an accounting of his crops and livestock in order to receive compensatory units from the state for his labor. Likewise with our fishers and hunters. But still the—"

"I do not eat pequium meat," Yeardance interjected.

"Nor do I. Nor do any of us." Durane patted his hand—a bit of tactile laughter for the not very funny joke he had made. "Discounting pequia, Tezcatl has a number of indigenous species which *are* edible, you see, and we have introduced forms," holding up a piece of braised coney in her chopsticks, "that have prospered here, even outside breeding kennels and laboratories. But one must be of an independent and assiduous mind to be a hunter on our world, I think, and civkis licensed for this task are few, relatively noted. Many hunters are 'fallaways' who live as hermits and keep their catch to themselves, and we can't hope to regulate them in their . . . egoistic hermitages. Isn't it always so, when a colony grows up too far?"

"The idea of colonies is that one day they will grow up 'too far.' "

"Yes. But isn't it lamentable? One's early hopes go through their realization to a joy foreseeing its own collapse. Today Tezcatl has its forward-looking joy, and wouldn't it be good if only we could preserve it?"

Jaeger, a dustbowl of the spirit, had never attained the joy Bursar Durane spoke of; it hadn't been made for that sort of attainment. And so Yeardance had gone out from it. . . .

"What I'm attempting to say, kommissar, is that we

can distribute only the commodities that come into our clearinghouse for the Smoking Mirror region. We can't distribute those that do not come in. That's obviously tautological, but I want you to understand."

In the darkness below them the soft ominous thudding of a tom-tom was heard, very like a heartbeat.

Over this Durane said, "My lieutenants insure that those institutions having a top priority receive their allotments without fail, often from the Komm-imports on hand. It's my job to be certain this is done. When we have worked through the fleet imports, augmenting various allotments with commodities that can only be produced locally, we must turn exclusively to our local products for low-priority 'disbursements.' Understand?"

This was all terribly nonspecific and uninteresting, Yeardance felt—but he believed he saw the woman's point, even through the mustard-yellow fog rising in his head. The heartbeats from the well made this fog pulsate. . . .

"You've finished your drink. Do you want another?" As soon as she had asked, it seemed, a new one was in his hand.

" 'Sar Yeardance, the truth is, there is corruption on Tezcatl. Already. Even, you see, as we are between our infancy and our unformed adulthood. The self-conscious cynicism of adolescence. No, no, don't anticipate me—I don't mean Governor Entrekin. For the most part our Komm-appointed officials—all of whom are native—are industrious and upright, even if we do have our share of mean and self-serving personalities. These we contain well, I think. But the cynicism of those who reside outside our managerial checks and balances, well, in some cases this impinges on our ability to act, and the corruption seems to be ours when in fact we are suffering from the irresponsibility of the very citizenry we desire to serve. A small *fraction* of this citizenry, I should qualify. Tezcatl is a good place, and the Tezcatli themselves are of a generous sentiment—if you understand a generosity defined in part by hardship and adversity."

He was going to say, "I think I do," but the tom-tom heartbeats grew louder and louder, and the *orkhēstra* was suddenly spotlighted from three directions by overlapping circles of red.

Gazing down, Yeardance saw two men dressed in loincloths and feathers jump into the overlapping spots. Silverware ceased rattling, and Durane herself turned her attention to the "floor show." The dancers' backdrop was the tall opposite wall of the Xipe Totec, and in its center, worked in antique-gold foil, was a large circular emblem bearing upon it a crude bas-relief jaguar. A round stone, displaying this same symbol but tilted like an askew tabletop, sat at the base of the wall, and the two feathered warriors began to stalk each other in front of it. Yeardance sipped at his rum.

Durane whispered, "It's a reenactment of a Meshi'ka campaign against the Huaxtecans during the chieftaincy of Moctezuma Ilhuicamina. Circa 1460, I believe. A.D., you understand?"

This meant nothing to Yeardance, but he watched as the men, carrying shields and clubs, circled cautiously in front of the jaguar stone. Soon he realized the dancers were not demonstrating how the Meshi'kan and the Huaxtecan sought to kill each other, but rather how they attempted to effect a capture. The capture was all important. The dancers swung their clubs in stylized arcs at each other's feet, and the tom-tom heartbeats counterpointed the rhythmic music of

their bodies. At last the Aztec warrior—his shield bore
an archer, symbol of his king—captured the Huaxtecan, who wore, in addition to the plumage of a soldier, an incongruous conical hat. Meanwhile, the
heartbeats grew fainter and finally ceased. Both dancers set aside their weapons and faced the audience of
the Xipe Totec, the captive kneeling in front of his
captor.

CAPTOR: Now, Huaxtecan, you are my beloved son,
          Whom the Flayed God wishes for his own.
CAPTIVE: Beloved father who gives me to the stone,
          O Arm of Montezuma, take me home.

The spotlights died on this tableau, and Yeardance
was momentarily disoriented by the sudden flow of
darkness in the bistro's well. A primitive sort of entertainment, he judged this performance—skillfully done
but affording none of the resonances of formal drama.

"That's the first scene," Durane said. "You're not
eating. Another drink?" The drink appeared, and she
resumed her previous topic: "I'm sorry to have approached this subject in such a roundabout way, kommissar. I should tell you that the cynicism I've men-
tioned manifests itself—in one of its guises, at least—as
a thriving black market in both essential commodities
and luxuries. And it is locally produced goods, of
course, that flow into the black market, and are hence
lost to official channels of priority distribution. This is
one of the reasons, 'Sar Yeardance, that our own *patshatl* runs to the Sancorage do not contain the types and
quantities of goods you desire. Our own people are
stealing from one another, and so the result is that we
can supply your 'low-priority' muphormosarium with
only . . ."

"Leftovers."

"Yes, kommissar, that's accurate enough, and I'm pained by it. The failure to fill our quota of goods for each recipient reflects on *my* performance, you see, as well as deprives deserving institutions of needed commodities. The reflection on my performance is of course secondary to the hardships worked by the deprivation of goods, but I'm professional enough to be disturbed—*and* pained—by both, kommissar." Her food was gone. She sipped at a cup of lidded theobromine.

"Maybe," he said, groping out of the tangled explanation she had given him, "the priorities ought to be changed."

"That may well be true, but I don't have the authority to rearrange them, even should I clearly see the need."

"Who does?"

"Governor Entrekin, or the Cadre of Four who advise him."

Yeardance made an asymmetrical loop with one finger. "Around and around. He sends me to you. You send me to him." He heard the invisible tom-tom again; this time the thuds were not heartbeats at all but the regularly spaced punctuations of a death march.

"It's not a deliberate technique of deflection, kommissar. The Governor isn't aware of the intricacies of my bursarship, you see. He told you to come to me in the hope I could help you; he simply couldn't foresee my response, taken with concerns of greater moment as he is."

"All right." Yeardance ate a cube of meat. "All right. Then couldn't we try to subscribe aid from private citizens, if you don't have the means of providing it through official channels?"

" 'Sar Yeardance, most 'private' citizens are supplied through the institutions that *we* supply, do you see? No one has a surplus."

"But no one is—"

"The second scene," Durane said. She held her chopsticks to her lips.

Had she known that he was going to say, "But no one is starving, either"? No, she was a sincere, a concerned woman—even if she spoke in terms that distanced these qualities. The argot of a bureaucracy, after all, was as infectious as any disease, and it was fortunate that her heart assured her a degree of immunity. "This scene," she said, "is the gladiatorial death of the sacrifice victim."

Circles of red began moving across the dancing floor, and Yeardance watched as the captive from the previous scene entered. He was almost unrecognizable. Instead of his duncelike hat he wore only feathers on his head, and was naked but for his loincloth and a coat of white chalk on his face and body. A new performer—representing a Meshi'ka priest—entered beside the captive and gave him a gourd supposedly containing the sacred drink *pulque,* made from the agave.

"*Pulque,*" Durane whispered, "was reserved by Aztec sumptuary laws for the upper classes. It was a crime for commoners to drink it—unless they'd been captured in war and were about to be sacrificed."

Four times the prisoner below them lifted the gourd, as if toasting his gods, and then drank. Yeardance toasted the dancer and, amused by the opportunity, also drank. Then the priest took the gourd, gave the captive a shield and a club equipped with four bolas, and leaped away as the tom-tom's beating grew steadily more frantic. A discordant stringed instrument sounded.

Four Meshi'ka gladiators entered—two dressed as eagles, two as either jaguars or ocelots. Their clubheads were embedded with wicked-looking obsidian blades, and they executed a series of complicated jumps and circling steps featuring quite dangerous maneuvers with their clubs. The spectacle was genuinely fascinating now, and Yeardance found that his head seemed clearer. When the first of the Aztec gladiators closed with the ashen-white captive, however, he saw that his right hand was clutching the tier railing with painful force. He released his grip.

The Huaxtecan captive gracefully dispatched the first eagle avenger sent against him, and then the second, just as gracefully. But the first ocelot warrior parried and thrust with consummate skill, and the two dancers whirled about each other like psychological polarities given flesh, neither one able to decisively overcome the other. At last, however, the captive slew this third warrior, and the second ocelot gladiator—the final one of the four—came forward with a fury that the captive was no match for. The choreography of his weariness was baroquely stylized, and he fell beneath a lacerating blow of the ocelot warrior's club. Then the Meshi'ka victor threw aside his warrior's accoutrements and intoned:

> Ilhuicamina, Archer of the Skies,
> Prevails against the courage, *pulque*-fed,
> Of captives sacrificed before his eyes
> And for the Flayed God, Xipe Totec, bled.

Darkness again. The image Yeardance retained was of three brightly bedecked corpses and one chalk-white one lying in unlikely but beautiful postures while a fourth figure orated above them, like a survivor at the conclusion of a Jacobean tragedy. The drumbeats had stopped.

"And even if we tried to enlist the aid of individual Tezcatli," Durane said, as if no gap in their conversation had occurred, "I would be uncertain of their response."

"Because the aid is for muphormers?"

"Yes. A prejudice exists. And a fear."

He wanted to say that his people were no longer muphormers at all, but the Governor had advised—no, *ordered*—him not to. Most of his dinner was still before him, and Bursar Durane was unsteady in his vision. "And you, bursar?" he asked her. "Are you prejudiced against these people we penalize with our priorities?"

"If I were, it wouldn't affect how we distribute goods to the Sancorage."

"I understand. But are you? Predisposed against them, I mean. Do you think it would be good if they all simply died?"

"Every Tezcatli is predisposed against them, to some extent. We grow up with effigies of their heads over our beds. And once, during Ebarres's kommissariat, I went out to the Sancorage myself, 'Sar Yeardance—with extra goods, you ought to know—to see this fearsome place. I even went on a *patshatl* run, with a civki who's since been transferred off-planet. Although we had enough food packets for everyone, I saw people beat others to obtain a *second* packet and I saw people laugh to see these beatings inflicted. I can't say that disease is the cause of such behavior,

'Sar Yeardance, because that would mean we require armed personnel in our hospital wards. So I am—as you would put it—prejudiced against what I have seen and been told of."

"Pressures," he began. "Pressures such as make your ideas of hardship and adversity seem inconsequential. It's all—"

"Another thing, kommissar: I visited in the summer, when it's possible for the muphormers to plant *centli* gardens, to breed coneys. My office has several times provided them with seed and breeding stock for just these purposes. But when I visited, kommissar, I saw untended garden plots in which grain was withering in the heat, unharvested. And I learned from my driver that the family of the muphormer leader had taken all the coneys for its own use, skinned and cooked these, and then made themselves ghastly sick on a barbarous all-day feast. So the arguments of 'pressures' somehow don't impress me, you know—as much as I would like to sympathize with their plight."

The *orkhēstra* filled with shifting crimsons, the foil emblem glinted, and on the stone table in the well the "dead" captive was spreadeagled with thongs about his wrists and ankles. The dancer's head was hooded, and he wore a skin-tight body-suit with limp cloth genitals to heighten the illusion of nakedness. Yeardance wondered why, if the effect desired was one of utter vulnerability, the performer had worn a garment at all. Obviously Town Tezcatl had no statute prohibiting the *emulation* of nakedness. Why, then, would its laws proscribe the real thing?

"This is the last scene, 'Sar Yeardance. Sacrifice and homage to Our Lord of the Flayed God, Xipe Totec."

"For whom the bistro's named?"

"Yes. An Aztec god of agriculture; also of spring.

The Indians sometimes called him the 'Red Tezcatli-poca.' Hence, the lighting for these performances." She beckoned to a woman in white cottons, and Yeardance found another drink in his hand.

A performer representing a second Meshi'ka priest solemnly entered; he came out to no accompaniment but the breathing of his audience. The heartbeats Yeardance heard now were his own, and despite the amateurishly suggested "nakedness" of the priest's victim he was compelled to watch as if this were not a reenactment at all but a kinetic retrochronogram of the actual event. The priest had an obsidian knife, and he stalked about the sacrificial stone holding it aloft and singing in a wordless, weirdly inflected moan. Then he halted behind his spreadeagled victim.

A drum thudded once, startling Yeardance.

The priest plunged his knife over the captive's head and into his breast. Blood sprang forth, crimson in the shifting spotlights, and the priest made a sidelong slashing incision from which, dropping the knife, he pulled out the victim's miraculously living heart. (Where had logic gone? The victim was supposed to be dead, but his heart was still alive.) The heart, held up, glistened and beat—*pa-pum, pa-pum, pa-pum*— like a flayed baby rabbit. Then the priest whirled away, the tom-tom mocking the beat of an adrenaline-fed human heart.

*Pa-pum, pa-pum, pa-*PUM . . .

Yeardance's own temples were pulsating. It was a moment or two before he realized the "blood" was colored water and the "heart" probably only an inflatable plastic bladder. Even so, he couldn't steady his trembling hands. Maybe now the priest would recite a verse ending all this. . . .

Instead the priest returned from the parquet circle

under the dining tiers and stalked his twice-murdered victim again. He stropped his obsidian blade on his palm and moved in.

And now Yeardance understood why the performer tied down to the stone had worn a body-suit rather than gone naked: the priest was now stripping the body-suit away as his victim's "skin," revealing the man's genuinely naked body painted so as to give the impression of raw musculature and the maplike patterns of exposed veins. The illusion was total, and therefore just as unsettling as discovering the blind Mari-shru trying to eat a food-packet wrapper with the nubs of her hands. . . .

But that was reality. This was . . . *what*?

The priest pulled the body-suit off his victim and donned it, stepping into it as if it were an oddly cut cape. He then unhooded the flayed man, stripped away the flesh of his face with his knife (it was a latex mask; *only a mask*), and put this on too. The victim's real features were made up to resemble a death's-head, and lying there in the reds of the spots he was an incarnadine study, a focus for his audience's sophisticated horror. The priest came to the front of the stone, lifted his arms, and recited the epilogue Yeardance had been waiting for:

Tezcatlipoca, in your red incarnation,
This captive comes home to you. Face to face

In a clouded mirror, O mighty, we petition
You to grant to us another cycle's grace.

I wear my brother's skin; I wear his face.
Who am I but he? Who are You but us . . . ?

"What does it all mean?" Yeardance asked the bursar. The well had filled with darkness again, and his
head was fuzzy with this new adjustment.

"The Meshi'ka believed the world had been created
four times before and that it was doomed to die
again, you see. Blood sacrifice couldn't prevent its destruction, but could . . . delay it . . . through the
magnitude and sincerity of the sacrifice, I suppose.
That's why most victims went willingly to their
deaths—they believed they helped their people by *de-
laying* the inevitable. Captor and captive each gained
honor through the other."

"But only the captive had to die?"

"Yes. Until another day, perhaps; another battle.
Then the former captor might be taken and it would
be his fate to propitiate Xipe Totec, or Tezcatlipoca,
or maybe Huitzilopochtli, with his death."

"A lovely fate."

"You haven't finished eating."

"Unless one is a cannibal the bistro's entertainment
isn't terribly conducive to good appetite."

"You weren't eating before the performance began.
And you can see that my appetite wasn't seriously im-
paired."

"I'm sorry," Yeardance said. "A thoughtless remark.
Forgive me. It's just that food—food is a distraction
from my main concern. . . ."

"I've tried to tell you what I could, kommissar. But
although I'm not altogether opposed to increasing the
Sancorage's allotment, circumstances don't permit it—
as frustrating as this is to both of us."

Yeardance tried to sort out the essentials. Wasn't
there something else he wanted to ask? He was drunk.
He fought his drunkenness back. "Chapanis," he said.
"What can you tell me about Kommissar Chapanis?"

"The woman before Ebarres?"

"Yes."

"I was a young understaffer in the bursary when she arrived, and I can tell you only that she made her presence on Tezcatl conspicuous by the public nature of her activities. I believe she contacted Albo—who was then the bursar—in the first year of her kommissariat, just as you have contacted me. She appealed for more goods, and received them. Later she appealed for still more aid, and was granted a small concession even though we didn't have the wherewithal to accommodate her as fully as she liked. When her demands continued, however, Bursar Albo and Governor Mann took steps to keep her situated at the Sancorage."

"House arrest, as Entrekin has likewise arranged for me?"

"No. She wasn't at first confined to the Sancorage buildings—she had access to all the Tezcatlipoca Reserve, just as you do, I believe."

"But she spent a portion of her kommissariat as a prisoner of her own staffers. Not so?"

"Very much so, 'Sar Yeardance."

"Why?"

"When she could not obtain what she wanted through official channels she ignored the decrees confining her to the Reserve, came stealthily into Town Tezcatl, and arranged goods shipments with the *dingoes*—the black marketeers, you see. She bartered away several Komm-service vehicles for these illicit commodities, as well as medicines and drugs. Her Civkis, we think, were told that these items were being requisitioned by Komm-service for use in Tezcatl's mining operations. Chapanis may have drawn upon her own private wealth, also, as a means of payment—although this would have benefited only those *dingoes* who could contrive to get off-planet to enjoy gains not negotiable here. A clever and valiant woman, deserving of at least a degree of admiration. Her activities were discovered only when a pair of her contacts were apprehended in the possession of a Sancorage carrier—they subsequently confessed their dealings with her."

"In what year was this?"

"The fourth or fifth one of her kommissariat. She was detained in the Sancorage's admin quonset for the last two or three years of her extended assignment. But even during these years, we think, *dingo* items were delivered to the Reserve for the muphormers. Chapanis wasn't deterred by adversity, you see, and we don't know how she did it. Only when she was replaced by Ebarres did things return to normal."

"And the muphormers began starving once more." Saying this, he was all at once embarrassed by his own bitterness. He didn't apologize. Down in the well of the Xipe Totec he saw the image of the Meshi'ka priest dressed in the skin and face of his victim and holding up to the implacable gods a beating human heart. If the sight hadn't been an illusion, Yeardance would have put out his hands to accept it. . . .

NINE

Varieties of Murder

Durane helped him get back to the kommondorm that night. He remembered very little of his movements through the capital after leaving the Xipe Totec, but what he did recall was unsettling—Governor Entrekin floating through the fog in his head with a mask in his hands and something that wasn't illusory at all. Something very real . . .

On Sciarlin Street people were shouting. A number of Komm-service personnel came running from the lagoon, driving something languid and ungainly before them. They appeared just below the lift-chair platform at the head of the street, and a pequium—its jointed legs elbowing in and out—mounted the platform's steps. Once up there, it peered down the street toward Yeardance and Durane with slitted pupils and glistening containing matter. The beast's flanks rippled with wetness.

"Up on the platform!" a man shouted.

"They're not allowed on the island," Durane said, "but sometimes they swim across and come into the city."

Was this real! *The* real? The kommissar cocked an eye at the pequium; he watched as two men climbed the opposite steps and tried to push, pull, prod, and

shoo it down again. Laughing, the men were intent on
running the pequium back to the lagoon. People beneath the platform shouted advice, and finally a woman in enlisted-grade violets climbed the lagoon-side
steps and pulled at the animal's weighty rear haunches.
There was laughter and more shouting. The pequium
didn't budge.

One of the uniformed men made a gesture of warn-
ing at his colleagues and the crowd in the street. Then
he put a pistol to the beast's mindless head and pulled
the trigger.

The report echoed up and down the street. Yeardance felt scarcely touched by the sound, but he no-
ticed through its ebb that the pequium was still staring at him and Durane—its head hadn't even bobbled
under the cartridge's impact.

Another shot was fired. And another. To the same
effect.

People began coming out of Sciarlin Street's amusement centers; the avenue was aswarm with buzzing
voices.

A fourth shot made the beast's rigid neck collapse.
Then two more bullets were fired to dispatch it. There
was no blood, no reflex pumping of limbs—a death
entered into almost voluntarily, it seemed. It took
eight or nine people, some recruited unwillingly from
the crowd, to drag the dead animal down the steps to
the street.

Bursar Durane directed Yeardance away from the
pequium's corpse and helped him climb the opposite
set of stairs. Then she rode with him to the kommondorms across the island.

Someone—he didn't know who—saw him into bed.
He dreamed. But beneath all his dreams was his subconscious realization that the trip to Town Tezcatl

had accomplished nothing for him but a joyless ine-
briation. Nothing. Nothing at all.

In the morning the kommissar and Niemiec returned to the Sancorage. Yeardance wondered if he
had got a promise from Durane to deliver an interca-
lary shipment of goods and seemed to remember that
he had. He'd sloppily badgered this concession from
her on the chair lift. Or had he . . . ? On the carrier
ride back Yeardance worried this question to shreds.

When they arrived, however, they found Ambrogiani, Vowell, and DeLoach in their shirtsleeves in front
of the supply warehouse. They were carrying crates
marked with the bursar's stamp into the building.

"A delivery for the next four brace-weeks!" Ambrogiani declared. "The pilot told us—on Bursar Durane's
order, you see—that we must make do with this shipment for that long or else suffer when it's gone."

Yeardance, glancing around, felt that his stock with
Niemiec and the other civkis had gone up because he
had seen to the Sancorage's resupply. But for almost
four hours that morning he and young Anscom had
engaged only in dialogues demanded by necessity or
courtesy, as if the boy were punishing him for both
his shameful behavior and his failure with Town Tezcatl's officialdom. But now, bucking crates into the
warehouse with the others, Yeardance saw that Niemiec had reacquired his old animated nonchalance,
contriving to slouch even as he staggered under the
weight of a supply box. The boy didn't believe him
another Ebarres, and that was good, very good. . . .

"Now let's take some goodies inside to eat," Thordis
Vowell said, their work almost completed. "We've
been living on theobromine fumes and wet paper, I
tell you, for the last two days."

Were we gone no longer than that? Yeardance wondered. Aloud he said, "We could each take a food packet, you know."

The mirth of his staffers died and they regarded him with the chilliness he had come to expect as the portion of one in authority. Hadn't he reserved a similar chilliness for Michaelis aboard the *Night Mercy?* Yes, but it had come later—when both he and the captain had lost their respect for each other. Yeardance again considered the possibility that his civkis were filing reports on his performance. If they *were* filing reports, shouldn't he avoid estranging them with sarcasms? No doubt. But how did you achieve respect for yourself when courting others' respect entailed a conscious deferral to prejudice? This was all too abstract. Look at Civ Vowell's face. She'd meant nothing by her remark—he had twisted it into an unfair contrast. Well, well. He was back at the Sancorage and this was how it had begun.

"All right," Yeardance said, to undercut his last comment, "let's do as Civ Vowell suggests and restock the refectory's larders."

A bit of their former gaiety slowly returned, and the civkis dollied boxes to the hydraulic cage of the refectory. Soon they were asking questions about Town Tezcatl and their old chapter halls and even tweaking Yeardance about the stubble of beard he'd allowed to grow. "Has Niemiec corrupted you, sir?" "Is this the new style among high-ranking Tezcatl?" For them his mission to the capital had been a total success. The evidence of his success was in their hands, on the dollies they pushed across the yard.

Soon Tysanjer joined them from the infirmary and the celebration took on the aspect of a genuine homecoming. Hand-clapping, fencing bouts with phantom rapiers, irreverent jigs . . .

The civkis, Yeardance realized, were truly glad to see him, and not only because a helicraft had flown in at his behest—they respected him, as they could never respect a recluse like Ebarres, and all he need do to preserve their respect was have a little regard for their humanity. At the same time, the helicraft's visit hadn't hurt his standing. . . . What, though, would they think if they knew he hadn't succeeded at all? if they realized that the morning's shipment was merely a personal concession from Bursar Durane and not a long-term commitment? Only Yeardance knew the full extent of his failure.

"How are our patients doing?" he asked Tysanjer inside.

"Fine, I suppose," the orderly said hesitantly. "They're all of them gone, you see, but for the old woman they call the Radyan Maid."

"Gone?"

"Yes, sir. They got up last night—there were only seven of them remaining—and exited through the connecting corridor to the admin unit, sir. They went down the front steps of that building and returned to their homes."

"You let them?"

"No, 'Sar Yeardance. We found the door ajar and footprints in the dirt below the quonset."

"And who was on duty?"

Tysanjer paused. "I, sir. I was on duty."

"No, you weren't. Who was on duty?" The boy started to protest, his face as earnest as a full moon. "*Who was on duty*, Civ Tysanjer?"

"Neo-starb Zobay, sir. Gaea. She was in the infirmary most of yesterday and insisted on remaining last night. And dozed, you see. While she dozed they tip-toed by, these old ones." Tysanjer made a ridiculous tiptoeing gesture with two fingers.

"It was once the practice to shoot those who slept at guard, Civ Tysanjer."

The boy's face darkened, and Yeardance was amused both by this and by his own mental image of the muphormers sneaking out of the infirmary. Gaea *must* have been tired. . . .

"Is she there again today, Civ Tysanjer?"

"Yes, sir. When she discovered what had happened she refused to go to bed—even though I told her a legless old woman required, well, less diligence in the watching. My desire to console made her more adamant."

"So I would imagine." Purposely blank of expression, Yeardance was delighted.

Leaving the others to stock the wall ovens, he led the boy down to the infirmary. They found Gaea at her station, and the Radyan Maid sleeping with her face turned toward the wall. The girl's eyes were lined with a redness almost like wax, and the kommissar wondered if lack of sleep was responsible, or a bit of weeping, or a combination of the two. The shaveskull didn't seem the kind to cry over a matter involving duty performance, even if she regretted a personal error.

"I want you to retire to the dormitory," Yeardance told her.

"What other punishment will I receive?" She stood up.

"I don't believe being granted an opportunity to sleep qualifies as 'punishment,' does it?"

"I don't know, sir." And she didn't. Maybe she suspected him, as Vowell had, of sarcasm.

"Go on," he said gently. "It's warmer now, and if the muphormers don't choose to stay for treatment, maybe we shouldn't force them to."

Gaea Zobay left them without another word. Tysanjer took her place, and Yeardance walked down the aisle to the Radyan Maid's bed. He sat down at its foot, and the old woman's head lifted from the pillow and turned toward him.

The rigidity of her neck, the slits of her eyes, and the absence of either intent or interrogation in her face made Yeardance think of the pequium in Town Tezcatl receiving six bullets into its cranium at nearly point-blank range. The hideousness of both beast and woman derived less from their appearance than from the only idea implicit in their stares: "Here I am, and I am worthless." Yeardance also discovered for the first time a resemblance between the Radyan Maid and her son Pollo.

"Come you to shrive me?" she asked him.

"I've done that already, Radyan Maid, not even a brace-week ago."

"You didn't lift my guilt. It ain't been lifted."

He leaned forward and took her cold, papery hand. "Did you see others leave last night, Maid?"

"No, or I'da shouted for 'em to take me too, 'sar, or stopped 'em so's *they* couldn't leave. Dung they be for not taking me!"

Her eyelashes glittered with tiny beads of light.

"Do you know why they left?"

"Because a church be not to live in, 'sar, and the priest was gone, and it ain't no heartsease then. I want to go, too. I want to see my Pollo, who don't know how to cope along without his Radyan Maid."

"Surely Yurl Stofin will see to him, his own marriage-brother."

"Surely Yurl Stofin will look after hisself, I do wager. Just like them what snuck by me in the night. 'Nothing here,' they said, 'but the day before the kommissar did leave us, there was a *patshatl*,' they said, and that be why they've beat it back to N'hil, 'sar—not because they have a Dee Dum waiting."

"Is it likely the others will give them anything from the run?"

"Ain't. 'Deed, it ain't."

"But you wish to go, too. Only to see Pollo?"

"Aye, and the Burgeontide feast fast approaches, and then even the chidder swarms may for a time come home. Useless as I be, I will not spend my Burgeontide in this maybe-church."

"Another few days, Radyan Maid—until we've put some strength in you with our care. Then perhaps Yurl Stofin will take you home."

"Mari-shru do be gone, and ain't I stronger than her? You must let me go, too, or shrive me of my guilt with a death, 'sar." Like the claw of some wizened feline animal her hand clutched at his. . . .

A day later, in his journal of confessions: *Burgeontide, the vernal equinox, is a scant twelve days away, my people tell me. I fear it. The muphormers—who are not diseased at all anymore, if they ever were— look forward to the coming of the Burgeontide festival and term its celebration a feast. Why? They have nothing.*

Niemiec tells me that a few of the people have planted centli *gardens on the gentler slopes around N'hil and that some of the men have gone out hunting snow lizards (the snow is gone), imported coneys, and other scarce beasties. But the* centli *stalks won't bear before Burgeontide, and Vowell declares that the "chidder swarms" have just about hunted out the small game of the Reserve. She says that the people are just going through the motions of supporting themselves—soon they'll fall back on their innate lethargy and our handouts. Spring among them, she says, is a time of grandiose gestures and despairing relapses.*

"How so?" I ask her.

"They pretend to be coming to grips with their lives, and doing so seems to worsen their muphormosy—gesture and relapse, you see."

"They don't have muphormosy."

"Well, after the 'feast' of Burgeontide many of them come into us for treatment with antibiotics, people who haven't come in all year. That's what the records say, and last year we civkis saw it happen. And did for our patients just as the micro-codices on proper treatment say to do, though many of them would not let us touch them or look at them closely."

Therefore I fear Burgeontide. And I fear equally the casual indifference of these good young people to the mentality they have helped to create—or, at least, that they've fostered through their own unexamined prejudices. Which mind-set is the more frightening, our patients' or my staffers'?

Yeardance flipped back a page or two and read: *Wounded by others, we move to wound ourselves. . . .*

On his second day back the kommissar directed Niemiec and DeLoach to go down to the Compound and check on the six elderly patients who had contrived to escape during his absence. He was afraid they had received no aid from their fellows. Some might want to come back, but were not doing so because of the intimidation of other muphormers. Who could say? Yeardance was especially worried about the blind and lame Mari-shru.

The two young people were gone all day. When they returned, DeLoach—even though her face was flushed and her lower lip purpled with teeth marks— appeared more collected than Niemiec.

"Mari-shru was dead," the girl said. "Two of the others weren't in the Compound at all, and the other three argued that they didn't wish to return to our 'infirmary-church.'"

"Mari-shru is dead?"

"Aye, sir. Anscom and I took her body out of the Compound. Stofin and one of the Codwert men came with us, out of curiosity only, I think. We drove the carrier to the edge of a fen beyond the village and there cremated her with evapoflame, inside a bundling sheet—as the regulations require. Codwert and Stofin laughed heartily at how she burned and left before we were finished."

Niemiec spoke without meeting the kommissar's eyes. "I had to crush her skull down with my boots. Then more evapoflame. It took a long time."

Yeardance felt an odd relief—death and cremation were absolute kindnesses for an old woman like that. True, but his relief didn't derive from that reflection; it derived from the fact that the muphormers hadn't eaten Mari-shru's corpse. . . .

"Since we didn't have to return Stofin and Codwert to the village," DeLoach was saying now, "we came back by a different route—over a group of hillocks to the north."

"We didn't *want* to go by the Compound again, sir."

"No, sir. That we didn't. And in a copse of blackbuds—the quietest place you may imagine, sir—we found the one . . . the large one, you know. . . ."

"Dee Dum," Niemiec said, eyes to the floor.

"We found Dee Dum winched over a blackbud limb with a rope of vines, hanging there in the copse, you know, like a big naked baby." DeLoach's eyes suddenly fired. "They'd coldbloodedly murdered him, 'Sar Yeardance, one of the chidder swarms, and then drained the blood out of him with sharpened stones. The leaf floor was stained with it."

Yeardance's sense of relief burned away, as if with a dousing of crematory chemical, and he thought, Forty years he survived them, forty years—because he had a mother who could help him "cope along" in the midst of their infantile contempt. . . .

He eased himself down from the edge of his desk. "I thought Pollo was in Yurl Stofin's care! God damn it, I know he was! This is on Stofin's head!"

The civkis remained silent. They understood that the kommissar was raging for himself—not for them— definitely not *at* them. They watched as he paced to the quonset's opposite wall and turned with his face limned against a rippling plastigraph map. His face partook of the rippling of the map itself, muscles in his cheek planes moving of their own accord—until he relaxed and looked at them as if asking them to tell him that he was still sane.

"On the day we examined Pollo," he said, "didn't we release him to Yurl Stofin? Didn't we send him home with his marriage-brother?"

"No, sir," DeLoach said. "Not that day. Briefly he took a bed beside his mother's, and we finished many of his tests the next day."

"And *then* he was released to Stofin's care?"

"I believe so, sir. He left the next day, and his

mother protested his going. She abused both Tysanjer and Stofin most fiercely."

The kommissar exhaled, and DeLoach and Niemiec looked at each other—their superior, although still perplexed and angry, was satisfied that he hadn't been an accomplice in the castrated muphormer's death. He walked between their chairs and lifted himself to his desk again.

"What am I going to tell that old woman?" (Again they understood that he was talking partially to himself.) "My responsibility. Or Stofin's. *His* responsibility. Mostly this is on his head."

Then he asked them a direct question: "What did you do after you found Pollo's body?"

"Sir," Niemiec said, "we cremated it, as we had the old woman's."

"No other funeral? The Radyan Maid won't see him again?"

"The regulations require immediate cremation," DeLoach said. "As soon as feasible, that is. And we don't think Dee Dum—Pollo, I mean—had been too long dead. The stench was mild, sir, almost . . . almost sweet."

"And now," Niemiec said, "all you can smell out there, drifting up from the hills above the Compound, is the smoke. Evapoflame, sir, has a resinous odor, and it hangs in the trees awhile. . . ."

"Two dead in one day," Yeardance said. "If this continues, Governor Entrekin may soon have his wish."

To that DeLoach and Niemiec could answer nothing, and after several minutes of silence Yeardance thanked them for their efforts, urged them to take a well-earned meal, and smiled wanly as they left him to the after-hour desolation of his office. Dolor seemed to drift off his meditatively perched form like smoke trailing through a blackbud copse.

In the refectory DeLoach told Niemiec, "Ebarres looked like that sometimes."

"Well," Niemiec responded curtly, "this is different."

Yeardance didn't tell the Radyan Maid of Pollo's death that evening, nor the following day. But on his fourth day back from Town Tezcatl, Thordis Vowell, looking up from her micro-codex unit, saw the kommissar staring at her out of eyes sleepily afloat in their sockets.

"Come with me to the infirmary," he said. And his voice sounded pleasantly authoritative in spite of the supplication in his eyes.

"Are you going to tell her, 'Sar Yeardance?"

"Yes. And I want you there, too, Civ Vowell."

Thordis Vowell had little trouble keeping pace with the kommissar. She was as tall as he, and her legs were longer. Even so she wondered why Yeardance felt such a compulsion to burst breathlessly into the infirmary when for two hours that morning he had sat slumped in the cove of his desk, as inert as helium and depressingly weightier. . . .

Between the dispensary and the infirmary he halted and caught her by the wrist. "I asked you to come because I didn't want to do this alone."

"Yes, sir." Through the slit-window behind him she could see red and orange flowers where two weeks ago there had been only ice.

"But I had another reason, too—for choosing you rather than one of the other civkis. On one level, Thordis, my reason may seem a callous or a vindictive one. Callous toward the Radyan Maid, vindictive toward you. But I don't believe it is, really. I hope it isn't."

"Yes, sir." The inevitable response to a superior's vagaries—she resented having to say it.

"I asked you to come, Thordis, because of all my staffers you're the one who most strongly believes in the 'corruption' of the muphormers. I want you to observe the Radyan Maid when I tell her Pollo is dead. Observe her reaction. Understand? And help me comfort her if she requires it—because she will, she will."

Tysanjer was on duty, and they found the old woman sitting in a motorized chair in the center of the ward. Thordis Vowell took note of the Radyan Maid's blank expression—which arose, she was sure, not from senility but from an inheritable emptiness of soul—and watched as the old woman languidly powered the chair forward and back, forward and back. If she wept for her son's death it would be because she was older than the others and the chromosomal effects of the disease hadn't progressed as far as they had in later generations. Besides, muphormers were cleverly adept at dissembling. The kommissar's little test would prove nothing, and although she privately acknowledged the man's good intentions, Civ Vowell didn't care for the demeaning role Yeardance had cast her in. Observe and repent, he was telling her. Observe and repent. . . .

Yeardance asked Tysanjer if he had procured the motor chair for the Radyan Maid.

"Yes, sir. She was weary of the bed and I remembered seeing a motorchair in the warehouse. Isn't that all right?" Skerry felt much as she did, Vowell believed, and wondered if the kommissar had arranged his presence in the infirmary for reasons similar to those commanding her own. Probably . . .

"That's good," the kommissar said. "I'm glad she has the chair." He didn't give Skerry a speech about observing and repenting, however. Maybe he trusted the orderly to *deduce* why he was there to witness the impending melodrama. More trust than he had shown her.

And then Yeardance told the old woman that Pollo was dead.

The Radyan Maid very nearly pitched headlong out of her chair, forcing Yeardance to catch her and hold her to him while balancing on his haunches. When he finally got her situated in the chair again, she grasped her hair with both hands and pulled her head from side to side as if attempting to wrest it from her neck, all the while crooning an unintelligible song that struck Thordis Vowell as a weirdly lilting accompaniment to her frenzied physical reaction. The enflamed growths on her face looked detachable now, like the knobs on a metal cabinet. Finally Yeardance told Tysanjer to get a sedative and to "hit her with it quickly," and using a hypodermic tape the boy complied—the tranquilizer melted into the Radyan Maid's belly-white forearm and in only thirty or forty seconds her head slumped forward as if incompletely guillotined.

The demonstration was over.

Thordis Vowell saw that the kommissar was trembling with exertion. His face was swollen and sweaty.

"Thordis," he said, "you can go back to admin now. Tell Gaea I'll be along in a while."

Tysanjer returned to the infirmary station, and Vowell, her superior's drained countenance fixed in her memory forever, strode through the connecting tunnels grimly determined to forgive him for his presumption. This time she didn't see any orange and red flowers supporting on their heads a shadow of cloud. . . .

After supper, which he took alone in his berth, Yeardance found his journal of confessions. The Radyan Maid was sedated, he was sure. The civkis had all eaten together, most likely. He had some time. He put the journal on his knees and spread it open. How many pages did he have? Seven or eight, no more. He found a clean page and put the tip of his pen to it. What did he have to say to himself tonight?

He wrote, *If we learn at all it's less often from success than from failure. And the only failures that have educational value are the ones resulting from the active pursuit of some end; failures owing to passivity, on the other hand, may be so muted as to be undiscoverable. Unaware or indifferent to this variety of failure, we stagnate in acquiescence and convince ourselves that a life of inaction is as noble as any other sort. Whereas . . .*

"Whereas, whereas, whereas. If you were writing a poem, Yeardance, you'd probably begin it with 'whereas.'"

He tore the sheet of paper from the journal and tossed the notebook itself away from him.

The weight of the Radyan Maid's grief was upon him. He remembered the troika at his doorstep. "You know how to worship our god better," she had told him. Maybe that accounted for the general muphormer reluctance to stay in the infirmary—they viewed his staff's ministrations as a variety of worship and they felt unworthy of it. It was a negative kind of pride—maybe even a shame—that had driven those old ones out of their hospital beds and down the hillside to N'hil. Soon the Radyan Maid would demand to be able to go too, even understanding that Yeardance and his staff would be obliged by the lights of their blasphemous worship to refuse. . . .

But I'm done talking to myself, Yeardance thought. And he drew his feet up and sat staring at the floor.

Ambrogiani appeared in his doorway. " 'Sar Yeardance, I'm sorry to have intruded on you—a matter of urgency, however."

The boy saw a ball of paper on the floor and a cast-aside notebook. Linen tucked loosely about them, the kommissar's feet were bare. I *have* intruded, Ambrogiani thought.

"What is it that's urgent, Primo?" All that day the kommissar had called them by their first names: a disquieting intimacy.

"Sir, the Radyan Maid's no longer in her bed."

"Where is she, then?"

"I don't know. I went down there after eating and found her gone. I've come directly to you, sir."

"Who was supposed to be down there, Primo?" The kommissar got up, rustled about for his half-stockings, and began to put these on. An empty food tray was visible in his debussy, sitting squarely on the toilet cover.

"Sir, you told us you'd go down there after eating. She was sedated, you said, and we needn't sit over her like mourners."

The kommissar blinked. His footgear on, he rummaged about in a drawer, found a holstered pistol, snapped this to his belt. "I'd forgotten saying that, Primo," he said evenly. "Come on, then."

In the infirmary cage they found no one at all, and when they checked the hydraulic cage at the rear of the quonset they discovered it to be resting on ground level. Ambrogiani, sent back to the station, couldn't find the hieroglyph-embossed key for coding open the cage door. He reported its absence to Yeardance.

"She's taken the chair," the kommissar said, "and tried to go back to N'hil. Not long before you arrived, Primo, I'd been thinking that she would."

They found the reserve key and rode down. Ambrogiani saw the kommissar look first at the stars, not at the ground. Tumulus looked like a black glove thrust into the inverted bowl of Tezcatl's constellations, a giant hand greedy for gemstones. Yeardance's face was blued by the starlight. Was he going to move?

"Do your constellations have names, Primo, or only numbers?"

"Names, sir."

"What's that one called, then?" He pointed at a grouping of stars hanging above Tumulus like so many bright, actinic hooks.

"Ilhuicamina, sir. The Archer of the Skies."

"Apt. And that one?"

"Coatl. The Serpent.—Do you wish me to go get the others, sir, to help us find the old woman?"

"The feedlot's empty," the kommissar said, apropos of nothing. "Oh, no, Primo. Go back inside. I'll walk down to the Compound to make certain she arrived. I'd like to go alone."

"Yes, sir." The kommissar's eyes, lowered from the sky, now appeared clear and sane. Niemiec had said that Yeardance was shaking off the deaths of Marishru and Dee Dum. All right, then. Ambrogiani obeyed Yeardance and rode the cage back into the shelter of the quonset.

The kommissar turned and walked through the infirmary's intestines—a maze of tubing, generator housings, and sewage-recycling units. Ahead he could see the milkily intersecting slopes of the valley below the complex. Surprisingly, it wasn't cold, and he had no idea why he had snapped a pistol to his belt before leaving his berth.

Midway between the Sancorage and the domes of N'hil, the kommissar found the Radyan Maid's motor chair overturned in a declivity of flowers. Just beyond the upjutting frame of the chair's undercarriage two pequia were head to head over the woman's body— munching, he thought incongruously, like moo cows, their heads dipping down and then bobbing back up with an almost maddening leisure and amiableness. Caught between nowhere and nowhere, they regarded Yeardance and he them for several unreal minutes. Although it wasn't cold, the fragrance coming off the flowers was a chilly one and he raised his pistol almost as an exercise against this chill.

Since the pistol had an eight-clip and he the self-presence to remember that it did, Yeardance fired four shots into each pequium. He did so coolly, at an uncharacteristic distance from their wincing snouts and their indefatigable refusal to lie down and die. He blinded them with the bullets. Ten minutes after he had spent his ammunition, when the last of his six staffers had arrived to complete the silent semicircle behind him, the beasts were still holding their riddled heads erect and gazing unperturbedly around out of their sightless eyes.

At least, the kommissar consoled himself, I made them stop eating.

TEN

Law

It had been eight days since the last supply run to the Compound, and Niemiec reported early to remind the kommissar. Yeardance told him to arm himself, ready two carriers, and get DeLoach and Ambrogiani to follow them into N'hil's plaza.

Thirty minutes later the two blunt-nosed vehicles—the rear one loaded with goods—sat in tandem in the Compound while the village filled with people, some of them coming out of huts, some hobbling down the hillsides out of blackbud copses. The inevitable human buffeting began. Without a word to Niemiec, the kommissar climbed into their carrier bed. The boy joined the kommissar, and to attain a similar vantage on the crowd DeLoach and Ambrogiani climbed into the bed of their vehicle.

A sea of raucous deformity lapped at the carrier hulls. There was no reasoning with its incessant battering, no shouting it down. Always in the past Niemiec had given out two packets to the first muphormer at the tailboard, then slung the rest more or less haphazardly into the picketing of arms raised to him. Unless Stofin intervened, you could do little else.

Surprisingly, Lucian Yeardance found something else to do. He fired his pistol three times into the air—

so that even the wind rattling in the blackbuds was compressed out of hearing by the explosions. The crowd hushed, and Yurl Stofin himself came out of his hut to stare down at their convoy.

"Yurl Stofin!" the kommissar shouted. "Yurl Stofin, this is your *patshatl*! See how we've come to you!"

The muphormers gazed up at Yeardance; a very few, Niemiec saw, turned their heads toward Stofin, to measure his reaction to this unusual overture. The civki couldn't see what face the kommissar was wearing today, only that he was consciously over-mastering his trembling hands.

"Aye!" Stofin shouted, still taken aback. "Welcome, welcome! Do you bring heartsease, coming with two cars?" (The non/ent could easily see that one of the carriers was empty.)

"For myself, perhaps!" Yeardance responded. "For your people too, I hope!"

"Good, 'sar! Now that we do be quiet, give your giftings to whoever you do think fitsome!" Then Stofin turned to go back into his heathut. The wind abruptly died away.

"You'll have to come for your own food packet today, Yurl Stofin," the kommissar said, no longer having to shout.

"'Sar?" Stofin faced his tormentor again. Niemiec felt that Stofin was only now realizing that the kommissar had it in mind to humble him.

"If you wish a food packet, you must come down here for it. No one will be permitted to deliver one to you."

Stofin leaned forward, exaggerating the hump of his back, and cocked his head like a lap animal. "As our maybe-priest wishes. I do come down to you now, 'sar, for to receive my heartsease." Admonishingly bent over, digging his heels into the hillside, he started down.

"When you get here," Yeardance said, "climb into this carrier with me and sit down next to the tail-board."

The no-nose man halted. "Why must I put me in your car?"

"I'm bringing a new kind of law to N'hil, Yurl Stofin," the kommissar said. Although his hands were steady, Niemiec could hear a quaver in his voice.

"Law, 'sar?"

"By sins of omission at least, you're a murderer, Yurl Stofin, and as your kommissar I'm taking you into custody for the murders of Pollo Speck, your marriage-brother, and Mercy Speck, the woman known among you as the Radyan Maid, your marriage-mother."

The wind roared through the plaza again, but no one moved. Niemiec waited for a sign of astonishment, or resistance, or even approval to erupt from the crowd—but nothing happened. The non/ent and the kommissar were counterpoised like gods above the crowd's incomprehension. A crippled Red Tezcatlipoca versus Yeardance in the Plumed Serpent's incarnation as Ehécatl, Lord of the Wind. The old mythologies taught with such mocking offhandedness in the kommondorms of the capital had here taken on flesh. Finally the Red Tezcatlipoca relented to the Lord of the Wind. . . .

As the crowd parted grudgingly for him, the non/ent did as he was bid and hoisted himself into the carrier. No one struck him, but curses came down on his head in a flurry, and he slumped out of the crowd's sight by the tailboard. The kommissar trained his pistol on Stofin.

Chaos reigned again in the plaza, and some of the

young muphormers had started to rock their carrier back and forth.

"Stop it!" Niemiec heard the kommissar shout, unavailingly. Then Yeardance discharged his pistol, and the rocking ceased.

"Civ DeLoach and Civ Ambrogiani will distribute your rations and your heartsease.—Civ DeLoach, a packet for Yurl Stofin, please!"

The girl tossed the packet over her vehicle to the kommissar, who caught it against his side with his left arm and handed it to Niemiec.

"Today," he said, "packets will be handed out in a descending order by age, oldest first, youngest last. This is the way it will be on all *patshatls* from now on. Dissemblers will get nothing. Those who use force to advance themselves will get nothing. Does everyone understand?"

The faces turned up to him now were as ugly in their mistrust as in their mutilations.

Stofin, knees to chin, said, "When you go, 'sar, it will be the strong and mean what do take the packets home, the old and weak what must go without and beg mercy and food of the chidder swarms. This do be a useless plan you try."

"We also expect good behavior in your daily affairs with each other," Yeardance said, ignoring Stofin. "Your non/ent is in custody for turning out his marriage-brother, in violation of the Radyan Maid's trust, and for precipitating Pollo's death at the hands of your children. The Long Quarantine is not also a quarantine from law."

"*The Radyan Maid,*" Stofin whispered, "*I did not turn out, 'sar, nor her unfitsomely bedunged Dee Dum neither—I vouch it!*"

"Anscom," Yeardance directed, "take us back to the Sancorage.—Leda, Primo, carry out the *patshatl*."

The boy turned the carrier about and drove it from the village. In the vehicle's mirror he saw Yurl Stofin's face framed by chromium stripping and sky. What were they going to do with this man once they got him back?

What were they going to do with Yurl Stofin? That afternoon Niemiec stood guard over the non/ent in the infirmary while Stofin paced up and down, occasionally pausing to look at himself in a full-length mirror. The Sancorage complex had no detention facilities.

In the refectory that evening Thordis Vowell, who approved the kommissar's desire to make the muphormers responsive to law, suggested that they put the non/ent in one of the hydraulic cages. This could be done, she said, by giving him a chemtoilet, running the ventilation and temperature-regulating systems continuously, and stalling the cage itself midway between quonset level and the ground. The other civkis were incredulous, and Gaea Zobay wondered if her older friend had not developed a sympathetic case of the same dementia Yeardance had apparently fallen prey to. Zobay was a neo-starb, though, and couldn't bring herself to contradict Thordis's argument.

Despite the kommissar's presence at table, Leda DeLoach suffered from no such compunction: "And how long, Civ Vowell, do we keep this man in our hydraulic cage, suspended between earth and sky?"

"That's for the kommissar to decide."

"Which cage do you propose to put him in, then?" DeLoach asked.

"One not frequently used, such as the one behind

the dispensary. We halt the cage between levels to make it secure against escape, you see, and to keep him from disturbing us with any clamor he might make."

"*I* use the dispensary cage," Ambrogiani said.

"You're the only one, Primo."

Skerry Tysanjer studied Thordis Vowell for a moment during the ensuing silence. "What does this accomplish, this imprisoning of a muphormer? Does it establish a 'frame of law'? Much trouble is all I see from it. The muphormers are psychologically incapable of behaving, I think, within such a frame."

Vowell responded, "They are psychologically incapable of *accepting* the frame, unless it's demonstrated to them—as by this imprisonment—that they must. That's what I think."

Gaea spoke for the first time, because she had to. "What do we do when we run out of cages? Our demonstration, it seems, is over."

The kommissar, sipping at some wine Niemiec had uncrated the day before, had to put his glass aside. Previously he had been listening with a gloomy expression, but now he grinned and the table's mood shifted to accommodate his display of good humor.

"Construct a stockade!" Ambrogiani said.

"Death for misdemeanors!" DeLoach suggested.

Then Tysanjer said cynically, "We might inject offenders with the muphormosy bacilli, if only we could find a few strains cryogenically preserved in the Sancorage somewhere."

"Pray we don't," the kommissar said quietly.

"The *nenen*," Thordis Vowell said, nodding at Gaea, "has a point, of course. But maybe we will make clear our frame of law solely by detaining Stofin."

In the end the kommissar—plainly dubious of Civ

Vowell's reasoning—gave in to the proposal of his administrative assistant and agreed, that, yes, it would be good to detain Stofin for a time. As an example, if nothing else. To return him to N'hil so soon after taking him into custody would be to lose face with the very people who required a firmer moral leadership than Stofin either could or would provide. Maybe it would work, this detention. The kommissar drank more wine, and his civkis took diluted cacao-dope or simply ate dessert.

"I don't know," Gaea said. "We're too far from them, you know, for this to be effective. Too far." Which was very funny—she had never felt that way before. Before, further had always been better. . . .

With a recorder Yeardance interviewed the man he had arrested as an accomplice in the murders of Mercy and Pollo Speck.

Q. Weren't yóu responsible for Pollo when you took him out of the dispensary last week? Hadn't the Radyan Maid trusted him to your care?"

A. 'Sar, I do be but dung in the eyes of—

Q. *Hadn't* she, Stofin?

A. Aye, if you so suppose, my kommissar.

Q. I so suppose, Yurl Stofin. Can you tell me how it is that two of my staffers found Pollo's body strung over a tree in a grove north of your village?

A. They chanced there, 'sar, after Meedge Codwert and me went out with them to watch Mari-shru burn.

Q. I understand that, Stofin. But how is it you permitted this great baby to escape from your care—so that he could be murdered as he was, strung up and drained like a stockplant carcass? By children?

A. I put him, you see, in our hut with his sister Beatl, my skinmate. She was the one what had him to watch over—a baby as you do deem him, somewhat like our Teo. But Beatl do be all Womb-Beatl now, and has other tendings to see to. And so, in the night, Dee Dum did wander out looking for his very own nana, you see, and a chidder swarm found him on the way, most like, and said to him, "Come you with us, big one," and danced him off to the grove, laughing to find him alone. *(A short laugh)*

Q. And murdered him? Why?

A. For he do be fed by others, shoved aside at the *patshatls* and never hisself a forager. *(Appreciative chuckle)* A joke at my non/entcy, so you must see, 'sar.

Q. You think it funny, this "joke"?

A. *(Laughing)* Very fine, I do vouch you. So long did he last, 'Sar Yeardance, so painsomely long, and still the slitting did get him, no matter all our pains these many years. And they did want his blood too, you know.

Q. *(After a considerable pause)* Don't you see that the Radyan Maid would hold you responsible, Yurl Stofin? Since Womb-Beatl had Teo to care for, you can't shift to her the sole responsibility for Pollo's care.

A. If the Radyan Maid could be here now, I do aver she would be glad her shame be shed.

Q. Stofin, how can you assume she'd be—

A. And why ain't she here now, my kommissar? And why do you say I was a murderer of my marriage-mother when, it do be clear, she lay abed in the San-corage before her dying.

Q. I shouldn't have said that, Stofin. I should have confined my accusation to your role in Pollo's murder.

A. I had no role in Pollo's murder, 'sar. He did go out for that Beatl let him go, and *tlack!* the chidder swarm did slit him dry while he was wandering. His sister did keep him, not this non/ent.

Q. Stofin—

A. More a keeper of the Radyan Maid was you, 'Sar Yeardance, than I of Dee Dum. How did my marriage-mother come to be a meal for pequia, I must ask, when you did have her for the keeping?

Q. *(After a pause)* Stofin, that isn't . . . that isn't to the point. I'm trying to determine how you could have let Pollo go. It wasn't until she knew of her son's death that the Radyan Maid tried to leave the infirmary; that, you see, was what prompted her to try.

A. *(Laughter)* How well she did try, then. She did "try" as well as Pollo, he to go to her, she to go to him. Both the same. *Tlack! tlack!*

Q. You're confusing the circumstances, Yurl Sto—

A. *(Hollow chuckling)* Oh, 'sar, you do want me to wear your face, I aver, for even now you do have mine. I be dung, and you do want my face. *(Rising laughter . . .)*

The recorder was clicked off and the interview terminated.

Four days went by. The muphormer non/ent had a cot and a chemtoilet in the hydraulic cage at the rear of the dispensary. The temperature was kept comfortably steady, and Ambrogiani took Stofin his meals twice a day. Yeardance insisted on this, even though most of his staffers believed the muphormer ought to receive no more than a food packet for each eight-day period of confinement, only that and water. The result was that Stofin had more to eat than he had probably ever had in his life.

As for the kommissar, the civkis noted that he avoided the dispensary with almost obsessive single-mindedness, sometimes crossing the complex on the outside to reach the infirmary—he would by no means place himself in a corridor in the vicinity of Stofin's cage. Dementia, Tysanjer told the others; here was a man who had experienced countless slip-fix moments aboard Glaktik Komm's probe-ships, and the attendant demolition of brain cells postulated by Komm-service galens had to have a cumulative effect. Occupationally induced senility. That, in combination with Yeardance's failure to come to terms with the muphormers, could account for his mildly erratic behavior. All admitted, however, that he was still a far more appealing figure than Ebarres the Biliously Effete. . . .

On the fourth evening of Stofin's confinement, Thordis Vowell, dressed in a brown nightcoat, paid a visit to the kommissar's private berth. She walked barefooted through the tunnels, her hands clasped before her like huge translucent orchids.

There'd been a bit of pairing that night—Ambrogiani with DeLoach, Niemiec with young Zobay, Tysanjer standing aloof as usual because, he admitted frankly, he didn't care for the "oily mechanicalness" of sex. That had always been his attitude. Occasionally he could be induced to participate, but Vowell hadn't wished to expend the effort. Nor had she wished to suggest an arrangement of threes; the plumbing of it—"Who is this?" "Where am I now?"—could often be as tiresome as it was intriguing. And all she really wanted, at least for tonight, was to share the comforts of the flesh with someone as erotically melancholy as she was.

Who, then, but the kommissar could she turn to? In all the time since his arrival none of them had invited him to play, and surely his mind-set wasn't that of a touch-me-not or a pedophile. The man's alternating despondencies and enthusiasms must derive in part from loneliness. Why, many of her own did—loneliness, and the knowledge that at the end of Ton-attide she would be leaving Tezcatl, maybe for good. She and the kommissar couldn't be so very different. . . .

At his door Vowell heard Yeardance either pacing or tapping out a slow, arhythmic tattoo with the toes of his slippers. Then he made a hawking sound that reminded her of one of her male mentors in the Hall of Lysander. The strangeness of this made her hands tingle. She knocked.

"Good evening, Thordis. There, sit there." He wore a nightcoat surprisingly like her own. She observed that his desk was altogether free of papers, clothing, work supplies—as his desk in the console room never was. She saw, too, that he was holding in one hand the little plastic thetrode permitting one a tap-in to Town Tezcatl's aeolectic broadcasts.

"Just laving my mind," he said. "Wringing out the pity and the terror. What for you, Thordis, at so late an hour?"

Wasn't her presence—at so late an hour—explanation enough? "I wished to tell you, 'Sar Yeardance, you should not regret the measure you've taken with Yurl Stofin."

As he lowered himself to his bed, his knees peeping out of his nightcoat like two large raw knuckles, he looked at her sharply. "That, in part, was what I was laving away, Thordis. I do regret it."

She felt rebuked. "Sir," she said carefully, "you haven't had time to see if the measure will have any effect in the Compound."

"An effect on what? I'm afraid the tactic was a conscience-salver—that I've persisted in it this far merely indicates how desperate I am for answers. These people have no malevolent, infectious disease, Thordis—unless the human condition is to be considered pathogenic. Instead of detaining Stofin I ought to be petitioning Entrekin to dissolve the charter of these facilities and take the muphormers back into the life of your colony."

"Why do you not, then, sir?" Vowell, knowing how the kommissar viewed her theory of the muphormers' genetic inhumanity, resolved not to try him with it tonight.

"I did. And was rebuffed. And was told to stay put until called upon to emerge from my lamp. I am 'rehabilitating' myself, Thordis."

"Sir?"

"I am *supposed* to behave just like Ebarres, did you know that? Chapanis behaved like a missionary or an insurgent or maybe a little of both, and was punished for it. They confined her in this berth—they extended her duty-assignment here in the beautiful Espejo de Tonatiuh foothills. Even so, she managed to improve the material lot of her wards—by dealing with *dingoes*, you see—to the extent that they began having children again, not accidentally but purposively. Ebarres reversed that, though, and I'm supposed to walk precisely in Ebarres's footsteps."

He looked at Vowell in a way that made her uneasy. "I'm not going to do it, Thordis. I'm not going to be another stupid-looking face on the totem pole of Chapanis's predecessors. God knows, they must have been walking corpses, breathing their own decay. I'm *supposed* to be one of them. How Chapanis got in there, and how she kept herself in this kommissariat while raising such an idealistic ruckus, well, those are heartening miracles. . . . Do you know how *I* got here, Thordis, how I became your superior?"

"No, sir." Her hands seemed to have bloomed hugely in her lap.

The kommissar was looking at his feet, however, not at her hands. "I'm here because on the probe-ship *Night Mercy*—and please don't expect anything spectacular in this story, it's almost frighteningly mundane—I had a very gradual falling out with my captain, *my* superior, and at last offended him in a manner one might call 'insubordinate.' In lieu of a general court-martial, at which I would have been stripped of my epaulets, I was—as the flippant saying goes—'kicked down-stars.'

"You see, one 'twilight' duty-period in the command module of the *Night Mercy* we were riding the id-matrix, or whatever you prefer to call it, and Michaelis, my superior, was programming emergence vectors—but he was using scaler criteria to plot the points rather than the holographic values requiring a more involved computer run. The latter technique usually produces an imperceptible disintegration of the probe-field and a smoother reintegration into our happy Newtonian matrix."

Was this the sort of mysterious ingesta, Thordis wondered, Gaea was taking in through the alphodes? The kommissar saw her befuddled expression and laughed. She smiled and put her clasped hands between her knees, out of the way.

"Gobble, gobble," Yeardance said, shaking his jowls at her, and she heard herself laughing. "Oh, I know it sounds like gobble-gobble, and it truly is, to anyone sane enough to prefer the earth to stellar vacancies. —Here's the end of the story, though, the end of How Lucian Yeardance Came To Be Your Kommissar."

"Yes, sir," she said, accommodating herself to his pause.

He put a palm on the ball of each knee. "What Michaelis was doing wasn't against Komm-fleet directives, or dangerous, or even slightly reprehensible. Just *easier* than the other method and, sixty percent of the time at least, conducive to a bumpier, somewhat slower emergence. But Michaelis—there in the command well, with me and two second-grade astrogators, you understand—Michaelis *pretended* he'd been arranging a holographically derived program; he even positioned himself in front of the telemetric monitors relaying holographic data to *convince* us he'd been using the more difficult method. Thordis, I laughed out loud when I saw what he was doing. I said, 'Sir, a surreptitious incompetent is always found out. By their fruits do we know them.' I thought my tone was bantering and fraternal."

"And he pressed the articles of insubordination against you?"

"Well, right then, Thordis, Michaelis laughed too, and guided his command chair back to the scalars he'd really been working with. But bad feeling had existed between us for a while. He thought me addicted to alcoemulants (I was) and I thought him arbitrary and lazy (which *he*, in fact, was). What finally goaded him into impaling me on the code—or gave him the excuse to do so, I suppose—happened twenty or thirty minutes later. An innocent thing on my part, a ludicrously naïve request I would never have believed misinterpretable.

"My feet were hot, you see, and I asked Michaelis if he would mind if I took off my slippers during the *Night Mercy's* staged emergence. The captain must have regarded this an an arrogant affront, maybe

even as a swipe at the sort of program he'd opted for.
I don't think he was put off because of the 'unmili-
tary' nature of the request—we weren't spit-and-polish
fanatics in the command well. Anyhow, Michaelis
stalked out of there. Just before the 'night' duty-
period I was served with the insubordination articles,
countersigned by my own astrogator aides, who at-
tested to the truth of the 'Slipper Incident' even
though, you see, all command-well activity is dimen-
sionally taped in accordance with Komm-service
safety and historiographic regulations. Done in, Thordis, by my feet." He tapped them on the floor, the
same sound she'd heard before entering.

"Usually," she said, "it is by the mouth."

The kommissar smiled at her. "*From tooth to toe/
Our blessings flow. / And for different reasons, / Also
our malfeasance.* —I combine the talents of both ex-
tremes, young woman."

"Thordis," she said.

"Thordis," he acknowledged.

They stared at each other for a minute or two—
although Vowell was certain she and the kommissar
weren't really reading each other's intentions and mo-
tivations clearly. What was she to think of his story?
The kommissar of the Sancorage selected because he
had insulted a touchy commander by asking permis-
sion to work in his half-stockings. It wasn't funny, this
story—it was probably true. Thordis understood, on an
underlevel of awareness, that such a selection process
cheapened those who worked for Yeardance too; it
turned them into errand-runners for a Komm-service
discard. Did she wish to meld flesh with a man whose
fall had been a dead-weight drop rather than a me-
teoric plummeting? No hideous ruin and combustion

for Yeardance, only the slow seethe and the inevitable closing of a walk in quicksand. . . .

"Well," he said, "will you come over here, then?"

"Aye," she answered, all at once shy of her body, which loomed under her as conspicuous and strange as her hands had seemed to her earlier. She felt no shame at the prospect of sex, no lewd self-consciousness—but she wanted to apologize for being more imposing, more statuesque in body than she felt in spirit. Why? Here, duties aside, she and Yeardance were equals, in everything perhaps but age. She sat down beside the kommissar.

"Do you know any *dingoes*, Thordis, any black marketeers?" He put his hand on the inside of her right knee.

"I do not, I am quite glad to say."

"Ah."

Was that real disappointment on his face? *Dingoes* stole food from the very lips of the children in Town Tezcatl's kommondorms. And from workers. And from hospital patients. It wasn't hard to understand why Chapanis, despite her misdirected good intentions, had been locked up for abetting the colony's enemies. Couldn't Yeardance see that, too?

"Sir, what would you have asked me if I had said, 'Oh, yes, I know many *dingoes*'?" She put her hand on the inside of his left knee. A big, gristly knuckle of a knee. The fold of muslin bellying down between his thighs didn't even move.

"I would have asked you to put me in touch with the blackest of the lot, Thordis, so that I could be a . . . a Robin Hood, like Chapanis. So that I could sleep, you see. I've forgotten how to sleep."

"You wouldn't've done that, sir."

"Yes." The kommissar nodded his head. "Yes, I think I would."

Vowell started to explain to the kommissar that dealing with *dingoes* robbed the innocent, further corrupted the black marketeers, hastened the—

His hand interceded. It traveled through the wool of her pubes, over her belly's curve, between her breasts—to her shoulder, where with a bit of fumbling it succeeded in drawing back her nightcoat. She, in turn, drew his back. Looking at each other, they slowly lowered their bodies to the bed.

It all concluded, however, with Vowell's contenting herself with lying in the kommissar's arms because even with the best will in the world—tonight, at any rate—Lucian Yeardance couldn't do anything but hold her.

Three or four hours later Vowell slipped from the tangle of the kommissar's arms and padded into the console room. She had contracted Yeardance's insomnia. Her hand went to the touch-dent at the base of a louvered lamp, and a pool of light spread over the surface of her desk.

Her report to the Governor's Kommplex wasn't due for another seven or eight days, but she felt she already had enough to go on and the earliness of the hour gave her an opportunity to file the report while Yeardance slept. Later, the others would have to discover similar opportunities for *their* mandatory filings. The silent keys of the telescribe began taking the imprint of her report:

Lucian Yeardance has proven a capable and a conscientious administrator. His major failing, perhaps, is an unwillingness to withhold sympathy from those who do not merit it.

He has, for example, great respect for the unlawful manner in which Ebarres's predecessor, Candace Chapanis, procured supplies for the muphormers. Because of his ignorance of muphormer psychology (one believes) and of the economic underpinnings of Tezcatl society, he has a desire to emulate Chapanis's tactics. Unless he learns more about his wards and the colony which supports them, his ignorance may be a hazard to harmonious administration.

One must add that Lucian Yeardance is a humane man, who, even should he act in error, would not be acting for self-gain. This judgment, it must be admitted, would not mitigate the offense of disregarding legal channels of goods procurement.

A rating card had to be submitted with the written report. Vowell inserted the proper transit-negative into the console and electronically scored it. The negative even had a graduated series of ratings for a kommissar's appearance; she had always marked Ebarres at the percentile indicating "Slovenliness." Yeardance she rated only two graph notches from the top, tapped in her signature code, and transmitted the report to the Governor's Kommplex. In the morning it would be waiting there in a "developer well" for whoever it was who brought such things to etching-fine clarity and passed them on for action.

In the morning the civkis at the Sancorage discovered that their kommissar was missing.

Niemiec saw that one of the supply warehouse's lever doors was standing open and that a carrier was gone. The boy followed the carrier's tread markings beneath the tunnel connecting the admin and dispensary quonsets and determined that Yeardance was on his way not to the Compound but to Town Tezcatl. Why? Governor Entrekin had expressly forbidden him to come.

More and more irrational, Yeardance's behavior. As an example of this irrationality, they still had Stofin in the dispensary elevator cage, and although their prisoner had remained quiet that night, sometimes he bagan to yodel (with the gauze off his nose, Niemiec was sure) and startled them all into racing pulses and intestinal contractions. Niemiec had thought they might release Stofin today, and now the kommissar's disappearance had thwarted that hope—they wouldn't release the muphormer except on Yeardance's order. What did the man hope to accomplish, alone, in their capital?

At breakfast Thordis Vowell argued that he could not have gone far. "I was with him until very early.—Anscom, you might, I think, be able to catch him."

"And if I should, what then? 'Kommissar,' I will say, I suppose, 'come home to the Sancorage, please. Do not do whatever it is you're doing.' No, I'm not going to pursue him."

The day passed in spite of Yeardance's strange defection.

The only events of any seeming consequence were Ambrogiani's "feedings" of Yurl Stofin. DeLoach, who on both occasions accompanied Primo wearing a pistol, vouched to the others that the non/ent had shoved his food aside on their first visit, demanding to see the kommissar.

"I told him the kommissar had gone off on business," DeLoach reported at the evening meal. "He believed me to be lying, I think, but he sat down on his cot and stopped his pushing. On our second visit he took the food and sat with it on his lap, saying, 'I do be only dung, but I beg my maybe-priest's mercy. I must stop this too-much eating and be again my people's non/ent.'"

"'Why?' I asked him.

"'Two tomorrows it do be the Burgeontide feast,' he said. 'You cannot keep me here when on Burgeontide I must be home.' He wept and begged Primo to bring him no more food if only we would let him go."

"Aye, he did that," Ambrogiani confirmed. "He said he wouldn't eat again here if we would let him go."

The civkis laughed a little at this, uneasily, and wondered when the kommissar would return and issue the order of release. Even Thordis Vowell agreed it might be best to give Stofin his freedom—although she still felt that if their facilities had been less limited, the man's confinement might well have been the sort of deterrent to excess and cruelty that they were after. In her heart Vowell feared that in Town Tezcatl the kommissar would commit himself to a course of action that might forever derail any such experiments.

An hour or two before midnight, Ilhuicamina occupying most of the sky over Tumulus, Niemiec was lethargically moving around crates in the warehouse. He worked with an aimlessness born of expectation.

The kommissar had now had time to go into the city, transact his business, and return. The boy had a presentiment that Yeardance would be home before the Archer's feet wheeled out of sight behind Tumulus—but already lights were going out in the dormitory and so far he'd seen nothing on the slope above the complex but a foraging pequium. (Ever since the

Radyan Maid's death Yeardance had forbidden him to put hay in the feedlot.)

At last the supply orderly heard a growling in the foothills and picked out a spear of light lancing through the forest—then a second spear, and a third, and a fourth. Two vehicles! Niemiec left the warehouse and circled the complex to the point at which the carriers would emerge from the woods.

"Good evening, Anscom," the kommissar said when the first vehicle halted beside him. The boy started to answer, but the second carrier's arrival forced him to step out of the way.

Yeardance had returned under guard. Beside him sat an enlisted-grade woman holding a Phaëthon-47 half-rifle on him. She nodded at Niemiec politely when he stepped back between the two carriers. The other one contained two uniformed men, and on its sideboard was the interpenetrating-galaxies insignia of Glaktik Komm.

"Climb in, Anscom," the kommissar said.

Niemiec hoisted himself into the load bed and sat down against the tailboard with his knees drawn up to his chin. The two vehicles ground and clicked their way into the inner yard—a light came on in the dormitory.

Soon the kommissar, his supply orderly, the three uniformed strangers, and the other civkis, barefoot or slippered, were together in the admin console room. Watching his fellows arrive, Niemiec was reminded of the muphormers hobbling, limping, and shoving their way into the plaza for a *patshatl*. The same sense of suspended order ticked in his heart.

The woman with the rifle said, "This morning at the Tonatiuh Access checkpoint, one of our causeway guards prevented the kommissar of this facility from entering the city. This sentry, in fact, advised him to return to his duties at once—since earlier this morning all our guards had received an updated reminder from the office of the Governor that Lucian Yeardance was not to be permitted entry under any circumstances." The woman paused. "Sir, would you prefer to tell it?"

"No," Yeardance said. "You're doing very well."

Her thin face betrayed a shadow of surprise. "As you wish, sir." She turned to the civkis again. "We provided your kommissar with an escort almost a fifth of the way back to the Sancorage. He promised us that he would not return without invitation."

"We'd been ordered to extract this promise," one of the soldiers said.

"Your kommissar, however, drove down to the plain again and left his carrier in a brake on the southeast side of the lagoon. We think he walked the shoreline until he ran across a canoe operator beached there, mending nets. The kommissar asked this man for conveyance to the island, and the fisher—an elderly man, you see, who feared this stranger might do him harm— agreed. Fortunately he wasn't at all infirm of mind and he—"

The kommissar, clutching his arms, shook his head and giggled sardonically. "He delivered me to the guard at one of the checkpoints."

"Aye. And this time we escorted your kommissar the *entire* way from the capital. Now you see us here with him."

" 'Sar Yeardance," Gaea asked, "why did you wish to go to Town Tezcatl again—so soon after your other trip?"

One of the male soldiers responded, "His reasons aren't important. He must not come again. We've been ordered to tell you," indicating all of them, "that you are now responsible for keeping him here. Should he return again without invitation, *you* are to be disciplined under the proper Civi-Korps statutes."

It seemed to Niemiec that the soldier enjoyed the tinny preemptiveness of this announcement.

"That's true," the woman said, keying her own speech down as if to make up for the other's unpleasant fervor, "but perhaps you can make an arrangement with your superior that we could not—a promise he'll honor out of respect for you as his partners here."

She slipped the Phaëthon's sling over her right shoulder. "Kommissar, Governor Entrekin doesn't want a repetition of the Chapanis affair—which he believes his predecessor handled badly. If you should come to Town Tezcatl again and be apprehended, the Governor's aides have told us you'll be conveyed off-planet and returned to the Komm-fleet Judiciary for court-martial. And replaced by someone more compliant."

No one spoke.

At last Yeardance said, "It's too bad Ebarres was such a layabout. He would have liked that, I think."

ELEVEN

The Feast of Xipe Totec

In Yurl Stofin's face all she'd been able to see was emptiness, as if the gauze bandage weren't there at all and the hole beneath it was a port into an abysmal dark. But in the kommissar's eyes, at this late hour, she could still see the red and silver reflections of Town Tezcatl.

Leda DeLoach, a pistol on her hip, had volunteered to keep watch on their intransigent leader. Now he and Stofin were both prisoners. The kommissar had made no move to go to bed. He sat slumped in his coaster chair, teeth musingly clamped. Gaea—who'd been told to go back to the dormitory with the others—was also there, standing to the kommissar's left in a too-large nightcoat with a pictogram of the Aztec goddess Xilonen embroidered on one pocket.

At last Yeardance grunted. He looked at each of the young women in turn. "I promise," he said solemnly, raising his right hand, "that I won't attempt to go to Town Tezcatl again. And . . ." he halted long enough to grimace self-effacingly, "I promise not to break my promise."

"Why should you promise either of those things?" Gaea asked. She looked like an Oriental monk tonight.

DeLoach was surprised. Yeardance's promises freed them to carry out their duties as before. Did Gaea wish the kommissar to repeat tonight's fiasco? Did she wish all of them to martyr themselves to his adolescent idealism? Well, Gaea *was* an adolescent . . . more so than the rest of them.

"So that you can go to bed," the kommissar replied.

"I don't want to go to bed," Gaea responded at once.

"But I do, young woman. So I make you these promises. Tonight I release myself from your guardianship by making them. Tomorrow I'll release Stofin. We're both of us prisoners, you see, even with no one standing guard."

"We accept your word," DeLoach said. She was ready to end this baroquely disquieting day. The kommissar needed rest, too. . . .

"'Sar Yeardance," Gaea expostulated, "we don't *want* to accept your word. Did you go over two hundred kilometers today just to tie your own hands?"

"I went over two hundred kilometers today to no end whatever."

The girl's thin arms came out of her sleeves. "Exactly, sir. Exactly. Is it Ebarres who's come home to us?"

"Leda, take her to bed. No protests. In the morning I'm going to release Stofin."

"Yes, sir."

"And then we'll just have to see." He slumped back in his chair.

DeLoach put her pistol on one of the desks and led Zobay out of the admin quonset and down the corridor to the dormitory. She thought she could feel mute rage in the rigidity of the shaveskull's shoulders.

Like brothers whom fortune has separated, dealt with differently, and then reunited, Yeardance and Stofin walked together down to the Compound. A warm morning for once, Tonat as round and colorful as a citrus fruit. The red and orange flowers of the valley flamed at their ankles.

"Please, 'Sar, for you to see me home ain't a necessity."

"I *am* walking you home, aren't I? It's all right, Stofin—my penance for detaining you in a cage for five days."

"You may, I think, shrive yourself otherwise. Please go back." The non/ent's tone was devoid of emotion.

"I've earned your hostility, but its causes are now in the past. Ignore me if you like, but let me walk beside you."

The other man said nothing. In a few minutes they passed the spot where the Radyan Maid had fallen from her motor chair, at once breaking her neck. Here the pequia had had their short-lived feast. There were no flowers on this spot—the evapoflame had charred to black ash the corpses of animals and woman alike, burning a fire circle into the earth. Yeardance and Stofin skirted this circle, then hiked elbow to elbow the rest of the way to the Compound.

The village was empty. The heathuts resembled pieces of abandoned pottery.

"Where is everyone?"

"Roaming the forests or the valley fens, I would wager. Please go back now, 'sar."

"All of them? Everyone?"

"They do go out for the good weather, 'sar, the end of the snow. Some plant the *centli*, some dig up the brown-bottle tubers."

"Everyone? What of the chidder swarms? Don't

your older ones fear being split and drained dry, as Pollo was?"

"A great kindness was your walking me here. Please to go back now."

Standing in the empty plaza, the kommissar refused to move. A nervousness inhabited Stofin's eyes like a vision impairment.

"A truce we do have with the chidder swarms now," Stofin said at last. "No worry, you must see, of their naughtiness."

"*Naughtiness!*" Yeardance echoed.

Stofin faced away.

What a state of affairs. Murder was "naughtiness," and the foremost "nonentity" of a people who regarded themselves—at least by way of self-denying tradition— as "dung" had to speak of a "truce" with his people's own children! Weren't the muphormers, then, distanced from life by the very terms they used to describe its nuances and gradations? Yes. The kommissar felt he was thinking clearly again, although why he had insisted on walking Stofin down here escaped him. To do penance? Maybe. He feared it was to immerse himself in the irrationality of N'hil—all his other options, after all, had been blocked. And so, this.

"Stofin, what would you do if I were to return to the Sancorage? Wait here for your people or go out looking for them?"

"They ain't to be back today," Stofin answered readily enough. "They only just went out. So I would go out too, you see."

"Then I'll go with you."

"No. I won't go till you do plod on home to your civkis, 'sar."

"And I won't plod on home to my civkis, Yurl Stofin, until after I've followed you to your people."

The muphormer drew his narrow shoulders together; his expression geared down to a blank perplexity. He raised his hands, then dropped them. "It ain't for me to go, then. I will sit me down here till you weary of the waiting, 'sar." He hunkered in the plaza, arms around his knees, like a cave dweller in front of a· fire. His tattered leggings and balloonish sleeves disappeared in a blink of the kommissar's mind.

Yeardance sat down, too, crossing his legs and holding his hands in his lap. The two men looked at each other.

An hour passed. Two.

Stofin rose, walked between a pair of heathuts, and urinated on the wall of one of them. Then he returned to the plaza and hunkered beside the kommissar again.

A third hour passed. Shadows were stretching out like pieces of dark elastic. Stofin, groaning, assumed a lotus position similar to Yeardance's.

A fourth hour rose and set.

Stofin stood up. "Come if you like then, maybepriest. If one do roll in excrement, the dung be not to blame. Not even Chapanis would come out here, I must warn you, when it did come to be Burgeontide."

With that he strode through the village and gained its eastern suburb, where the bath and well facilities were, before the kommissar could overtake him. Stofin now seemed intent on shaking Yeardance with speed rather than patience—the benefits of his confinement were evident now in the strength of his stride and his stamina over rough terrain. The kommissar had done a bit of walking the day before, and his lungs heaved with this renewed exertion. Waiting Stofin out had been far easier than this. The no-nose

man was panting too, but he was breathing through
his mouth and doing so purposively.

After a time they came to a meadow with a peaty
underlay of decayed matter, and even Stofin had to
slow while seeking out firm ground on which to make
a passage. Yeardance, almost lost, realized that if he
gave up now he would have a hard time reaching either N'hil or the Sancorage again.

Once he saw a pequium on the bog edge. Later he
had glimpses of "snow lizards" (endothermic creatures in spite of their name) and an animal very like a
large pied rabbit—maybe it was a mutated coney.
Then Stofin led him into forest again, and he heard
birdsong. The distant *chirrup-chirrup* of these "birds,"
however, concluded each time with sinister rattlings
and cries. Everything among these conifers was scaly,
squamous with foreboding—light, sound, even one's
own thinking. Not once, so far, had they sighted another muphormer, adult or child.

"Stofin, how much farther?"

"To return to the Sancorage, my maybe-priest,
much farther than when we set out from N'hil, I do
tell you."

Very helpful. You didn't have to wait in Governor
Entrekin's antechamber all day to learn both hunger
and impatience; you could trek with the non/ent to an
unnamed destination and learn fatigue, too.

Finally through the trees Yeardance saw the colorful rags of N'hil's population—heard its mean, chitter-
ing voices arguing among themselves. All were here,
he was certain. The young and the old, the vigorous
and the infirm. The muphormers had apparently co-
operated in reaching this spot, a clearing on a hillside,
the anciently adzed torsos of trees thrown down to
make benches. Below the wall formed by a cut in the

hillock's face were three flat stones, each one large enough for four or five persons to stand on. The rotting benches were turned to give whoever sat upon them a good view of the stones. Farther up the hillside, among the trees, were temporary "dwellings" of brushwood and foliage, and the members of chidder swarms were darting about in the gathering twilight like dryads. The kommissar almost believed he had stumbled upon a community instead of an assemblage of egos insistent on their own worthlessness. . . .

Bare to the waist, Ino and Meedge Codwert came out of the crush of people in the clearing and greeted their non/ent.

"Aye," Stofin said, answering their stares, "the maybe-priest has come, too."

The faces of these men were far more grim than their disfigurements alone could account for. And for the first time Yeardance wondered if he had placed himself in danger following Stofin to this dim clearing.

One of the Codwerts asked, "Be he then a priest of Xipe Totec?"

It was Burgeontide Eve. It was a time of truce among the generations of the muphormers.

Stofin pointed Yeardance to a place where he could sleep and told a young man to give him a bowl of water and a half-day ration from one of the *patshatl* food packets. Thus Yeardance had two vitamin wafers and a protein stick, after nearly three hours of walking. The water was suspiciously dirty, and his attendant made a show of keeping back from him the candy bar and the pouch of instant theobromine in his frayed carry-bag. "Take the food," the young man seemed to be saying, "but don't hope for my hearts-

ease." Little wonder these people had developed deficiency diseases . . .

The muphormers avoided Yeardance while he ate.
They drew away and left him sitting on the smelly
cloak Stofin had given him for the night. Even so, he
saw people whom he recognized by name—all three
Codwerts, Womb-Beatl and Teo (who were now in
the care of Deeding worshipers unfamiliar to him),
Bruno and Elata Goron, and the Goron's daughter
Teá-bye. Many others he recognized by face or deformity, but no one chose to speak to him.

The kommissar realized his civkis would probably
believe he had broken his promise to them. What
could they be thinking now? Obviously he hadn't
taken one of Anscom's carriers, but they still might
deem him unstable enough to try to *walk* to Town
Tezcatl. Yeardance imagined the supply orderly
grinding through the foothills in search of him, two or
three others combing the Reserve on foot. At least he
wouldn't be returned to them with a Phaëthon half-
rifle leveled on him at point-blank range. . . .

Xipe Totec. Burgeontide. An evening with Bursar
Durane in the bistro on Sciarlin Street. What relation-
ship did these things have? Why had the Codwert
man asked if he, Yeardance, was a "priest of Xipe Totec"?

Intuitively the kommissar knew the answer to this
question—but he had been both living with and ignoring the answer ever since the week of testing and examination at the Sancorage, and tonight it had no
power to disturb him. Curled up in the cloak he'd
been given, Yeardance stared at the sky. Ilhuicamina
and Coatl gleamed through a frame of black needles
like distortions of the constellations he remembered

from his childhood on Jaeger. Finally his eyes closed and he slept.

Stofin was sitting over him in the incomplete dawn. "Drink this, 'Sar." He thrust a bowl out to Yeardance, who had to struggle to a sitting position to accept it. The liquid in the bowl was thin but milky in color.

"What is it?" Yeardance asked.

"*Pulque.* Or so we do call it. Drink."

Looking around, the kommissar saw muphormers moving through the trees like ghosts, carrying bowls, sipping as they walked. In the clearing behind Stofin steam rose from a caldron at the base of one of the three flat rocks there. Someone was ladling out the same fermented beverage steaming under his nostrils now like a sweet turpentine. He took a sip from his bowl. The taste was not unpleasant, although under the sweet smell was an herbal bitterness that clung to the teeth and tongue. When he had finished, Stofin went off and fetched him back another bowl.

"Stofin, I've had enough."

"Drink, 'sar, or you will be escorted home. This be the Burgeontide heartsease we do make only at this time—it must be drunk if one do wish to dedicate his-self to Xipe Totec."

The kommissar obeyed Stofin. The *pulque* warmed him. Even as its piquancy put him off, the numbness rising through him compensated for its scummy taste. The night's constellations had whited out, but he could still see several stars, all of them winking and fickle. When he stood up, Stofin had to take his arm. A tom-tom, like a pulse inside the last tenacious stars, began to go *pa-pum, pa-pum, pa-*PUM. . . .

"Come with me," Stofin said from galaxies away.

Yeardance followed him into the clearing, where *all*
the muphormers had suddenly magically congregated.
He sat down with some children at the end of a moist
rotting log. Noise. Smoke. *Pulque* on the children's
breath. A raw spring coalescing about them all.

Yeardance heard the non/ent say, "This be the
maybe-priest whose church did long ago fail him. He
comes today to see the worship of the lepers, I aver.
See you to it he ain't a trouble to us."

Disfigured faces grinned at Yeardance.

Where, though, was the caldron from which *pulque*
had been ladled earlier? It was gone. Indeed, how
long ago had Stofin come to him with two bowls of
fermented heartsease, forcing him to drink? He wasn't
sure. How had people gathered in this theater so
quickly, when only a moment or two past he had seen
the morning's first risers drifting *away* from the caldron with their bowls? His time sense was out of joint.

Now, an assembly. Sunlight burned through the
ground mist as a tom-tom thudded out a call-to-
witness. This sound abruptly stopped. Was it possible
that everything that was happening was an extension
of the sleep he thought he had just climbed out
of . . . ?

Beneath the hillside wall Yurl Stofin stepped to the
surface of the central stone and helped his wife and
child after. Womb Beatl knelt on the fore-edge of the
stone with Teo cradled so that everyone could see
him.

"A new god for us lepers," Stofin said, "for this be
the morning when the gods must change, if any such
been born to come against the old one. This year—the
first in six, you must know—the god to come against
the old one did have its birth to me and Beatl Stofin."
The non/ent knelt.

All about him Yeardance saw people go down on their knees, in front of their log benches. As a concession, he bowed his head without kneeling.

"The Feast of Xipe Totec," Stofin was saying, "must begin with the god what do be leaving us today. Teá Goron, who be Teá-bye now, must fall today from her perfectness in prayer to our Teo. Look you up to see, O lepers of N'hil, worshipers of this girl."

Still kneeling, the people looked up. On the left-hand platform of stone Yeardance saw the members of the Goron family, along with a man wearing a necklace of what looked like . . . yes, surgical instruments. So heavy was it, the necklace pulled his head down. On the central stone Stofin arose, and someone pressed forward from the audience to give him a similar ornament; he inclined his head to receive it. To the right, Tamara Codwert—already wearing a chain of scalpels, strigils, hooks, needles, and tweezers—mounted to the rock, and then hunkered down with her skirts about her like a pile of rags. These three tableaux crystallized.

At last Bruno Goron reached out and presented his daughter a bowl of *pulque*. The girl drank this and handed the empty bowl to her mother. The mother—"Womb"-Elata, Yeardance realized, until the Stofins had conceived a child—appeared to be holding back an emotion too big for her. Her eyes closed, she carried the bowl away and disappeared among the people in front of the three platforms.

To Yeardance the woman had seemed to float in an infinitely prolonged agony of suspension. It was the *pulque*, he was certain—the *pulque* in him, in Elata Goron, in everyone there.

"What do you give to fall from your perfectness in prayer to our Teo?" the man with the necklace asked.

Teá-bye held out her left hand. Her father caught her by the wrist and steadied the hand. Unclasping a knife from his necklace, the muphormer priest of Xipe Totec made the child ball all of her fingers together but one and then, striking quickly, hacked off the protruding finger with his knife—blood gushed forth, several people cried out, and the girl collapsed against her father. The priest picked up the finger and tossed it into the crowd.

"Our god be dead!" the people shouted.

"May our god live long!" came the response from others.

Womb-Beatl got to her feet and held her baby over her head. It began to wail—its coverlet fell aside, and its limbs rotated like a drugged shoat's. Meanwhile, the man who had severed the finger was now drawing a lesion line at one corner of Teá-bye's mouth, scratching it out with a blade and rubbing his dirty thumb into the wound to draw the pus of infection. The girl was probably only semiconscious; she hadn't screamed at the loss of her finger, and now her father was holding her up. Womb-Beatl lowered her baby back to her breast, and Yurl Stofin gave her a hand down to the clearing.

"In what leper's name do you baptize our fallen god?" the priest asked.

"After the Radyan Maid we'll call her now," Elata Goron said from the crowd, weeping. "Her leper's name will be Mercy."

"Teá, Teá-bye, Mercy," the priest said. He rubbed his hands together in the blood flowing from the girl's severed finger, placed his hands on her face, marked her with the blood. "You do be Mercy Goron now, ruined as we be ruined, unworthy of worship. Excrement with us, you must learn to be dung; you must

give the new god Teo all your heart's duties, if it do
be asked."

"And she must go out from the skinmates who made
her," Stofin said. "I do ask the chidder swarm what
killed my marriage-brother Pollo to take her in and
keep her living and teach her how to forage. You must
do so this year or suffer hard deaths at Burgeontide
next. Who of this swarm will stand for her?"

On the other side of the clearing a hard lanky boy
of twelve or thirteen stood up. "The Torrentson
swarm, what did bleed Dee Dum, must take the used
god, my non/ent." This announcement was followed
by derisive whistling and applause. Then, as if melt-
ing, the boy sat down again. Yeardance kept waiting
for an antiseptic and rational dawn. . . .

Now the priest was tying a spidery clump of moss
around the girl's wound. As he worked he shook his
head so that the instruments on his necklace danced.
Then Bruno Goron lowered his daughter to the
ground and leaped down after her.

As soon as they'd disappeared, people began moving about in patternless eddies. The caldron reap-
peared among these people like a breakwater in a
squally sea. Someone was ladling out heartsease again,
and another bowl appeared in the kommissar's hands.
He drank. The caldron vanished. Even when the muphormers had seated themselves again, he couldn't
find it. Were two or three of them carrying the pot in
and out of the clearing in order to refill it? What was
to be the issue of all this zombie-like wassailing . . . ?

The sun was up now, good and high, and he
could feel sweat rising through his soul like grease
frying off a rind of bacon. If this was a nightmare it ought to be taking place at night. . . .

Transfixed, Lucian Yeardance watched as during

the next several hours people filed up to the altars to
be newly mutilated. Many divested themselves of
their clothes and gave themselves naked to the knife.
The man who had hacked off Teá-bye's finger and
Yurl Stofin were competent butchers, amputating and
scarring, sawing and cauterizing. But Tamara Codwert was expert, it seemed, in cutting layers of skin
from rumps, under-arms, and breasts, and then arranging these in knobby grafts on her acolyte's faces. Under her hands "tubercles" and "lepromata" took shape;
under her hands muphormers were made.

Everything that was cut away was saved—fingers,
buttock halves, ears, toes, lips, everything. A mutilation rite more severe than the *o-kee-pa* of the ancient
Mandan Plains Indians. You could only believe, in
fact, that this spectacular butchery was a show—the
digits gaudy latex, the facial features merely putty,
the lean hunks of human backside . . . *what?* . . .
What could they be? Otherwise you had to believe
these people were deliberately abasing themselves out
of a conviction of their own despicability.

Yeardance believed this, and he didn't. He watched
pieces of these alien creatures being thrown into the
caldron—there it was again!—which had earlier contained *pulque*. Everything was terribly methodical—
an *abattoir* whose victims came sedated and smiling
to the slaughtermasters, in the bright noon of Burgeontide.

No, it wasn't noon; it was night again. Lifting his
eyes, Yeardance saw stars peering down through lazy
smoke and conifer needles. Bonfires were burning on
each stone altar.

Time hurtled by, but the motions of the surgeon-
priests and their victim-devotees were immeasurably
protracted. Tamara Codwert, it seemed, worked for

an hour or more at a time on each muphormer who
presented himself to her; Stofin and the other priest
worked more quickly, but with a stylized precision
that made their actions appear drawn out and endlessly graceful. Then, between eyeblinks, all three
priests disappeared and the altars were empty. Yeardance leaned forward to assess the truth of his own vision.

A child thrust a bowl of boiled meat at him. Another with a ceramic amphora poured *pulque* into the
bowl on his lap. Hungry, the kommissar ate. He drank
the fermented heartsease. Others were eating and
drinking, too. A picnic. A community festival. Oddly—
because of the others' fevered grins, their eyes
smeared away from reality—Yeardance had a dim consciousness of the horror he was participating in. It
didn't matter, though. His own face, he knew, had
adopted the same feverish imbecility. Besides, was he
sufficiently divorced from their aesthetic to disdain
what nourished them? No. He was among them. He
was *of* them.

Dawnlight again. The surgeon-priests were back on
their altars, shriving their parishioners of guilt and
flesh.

Where had the adults gone? Most of those going forward now were members of chidder swarms, and even
stooped over his knees the kommissar found that he
was the tallest of those assembled there. Even for children the mutilations continued. One of the altars
dripped with a mercurylike crimson heaviness, and
time pooled up in Yeardance's mind.

The adults were returning. With weighted carry-
bags people pushed their way into the theater. A few
held food packets aloft. There'd been a *patshatl* run
that morning, and the muphormers hadn't missed it—

even though Yeardance, their kommissar, had forgotten that eight days had gone by since his quixotic arrest of Yurl Stofin.

Someone filled his bowl with *pulque* and gave him a proteinstick, which he had no appetite for. He drank.

Later he stumbled away into the trees to relieve his bladder. Had he done this before? All he could recall was an eternity hunched forward on his log as the muphormers committed auto-sacrifice, ate and drank, and watched others do the same.

Who had delivered the *patshatl* goods?

Yeardance caught a woman's wrist. "Did my civkis ask for me when you went down to N'hil this morning?"

A face with a freshly scarred bottom lip turned toward him. "Aye, 'sar, aye." She could scarcely speak, but she smiled and tried. "They did . . . wonder where . . . you be, 'sar."

"What did you tell them?"

"Meedge Codwert said you and Stofin ain't come back to us at all, you see, and they do fear you dead." The woman laughed, her mouth open but unmoving.

Upon questioning, she told Yeardance that the muphormers had not come back to the Feast of Xipe Totec until the civkis had returned to the Sancorage. They hadn't wished to be followed, and after thoroughly searching the village the civkis had accepted Codwert's explanation.

"They did search it last night, too," the woman said, "if what that boy of yours spoke be true—but Codwert said we'd not been there because of our festival, you see. A few of us what did hurt the most went up to the infirmary to be cared for, and to see your people did not come after us, 'sar."

The woman's wrist slipped through his hand and it was night again, shadows strung between the bonfires like shimmering webs. He had to go back. He didn't know the way.

Standing, he saw the naked bodies of muphormers glistening as if their flesh had been oiled. His Komm-tunic, irrationally enough, lay crumpled on the ground behind him, and his own chest was bare. Demoniac faces nodded their approval as he stepped through an opening between two scaly trunks of Tezcatli pine. A man eating from a wooden bowl stopped in front of the kommissar and handed him a finger braised to absolute blackness in its own grease. Dazedly Yeardance accepted this, stared at it for a moment, and then gave it to a hand reaching up to him from the seated crowd. How was he going to get home?

Laughter floated toward him on the fumes of smoke and heartsease, and a heavy-breasted girl of fifteen or sixteen, clad only in a huge parti-colored skirt, her slack belly thrust out for everyone's beholding, stood beside Stofin on the central altar. Her eyes were haughtier than a muphormer usually let his eyes be. Stofin had worn such an expression at times, perhaps, and Womb-Beatl while holding little Teo up for "worship"—but no one else. And now the girl's eyes locked with his, and the message they contained for everyone was as transparent as the wings of a hummingbird moth.

She was pregnant.

Stofin halted the surgery long enough to make the formal announcement: "Kasmira has in her womb a god for next year." (He wasn't at all perplexed that the unborn child would be unsurping his own Teo's place.) "And for this Burgeontide, you see, we spare her from the knife. Womb-Kasmira she has become, and my Beatl must give up her name of utmost honor."

Appreciative laughter. A pocket or two of applause. Someone handed Yeardance a bowl of *pulque*. He drank. When he looked again, Womb-Kasmira was gone.

Stofin, with the aid of three or four others, was amputating the left foot of a conscious and curious muphormer.

"Once, two non/ents ago," an aged voice told the kommissar confidentially, "we did have a man what could take off legs."

"Aye," another voice concurred. "But now it do be only feet."

The kommissar sat down between these voices. Don't sit down, he told himself; go back to the Sancorage.

What did Stofin's skinmate think of being so soon shunted aside from her position of glory? Yeardance couldn't find her in the crowd. And the baby Teo . . . what of it? The Radyan Maid had said, "You do know how to worship him better, 'sar." He wondered if Stofin had fathered Kasmira's child. He started to speak, but no one sat near him to speak to.

Overhead, the inexorable ticking of the stars.

Next year, next Burgeontide, the Radyan Maid's grandson—little more than a year old then—would have to give up something "in prayer to" the god of the girl Kasmira. And go on giving up pieces of himself until he was an adult hacked and starved into a parody of a muphormer. Muphormosy. Three or four generations back his people had either outgrown or developed immunities to the disease, but the masquerade went on. Grafted tumors, the effects of pellagra,

and clumsily obvious amputations would serve to convince the indifferent authorities of Tezcatl that Teo
was indeed a "leper," when in fact what he really was
was a human being living under both a sentence of
excommunication and his own people's acceptance of
their pariahhood. To whom did one extend his
pity . . . ?

"Stofin!" Yeardance stood up. "Stofin, lay by your
knife!"

The spirit of the Red Tezcatlipoca, Xipe Totec,
laughed at him from the mouths of a hundred people.
Stofin regarded the kommissar across a seemingly un-
bridgeable distance, and when Yeardance shouted
again, he couldn't even hear what words he'd given
voice to. Were the stars already whiting out?

"Is it your wish to give up something in prayer to
our Teo, whose perfectness will be but short?" Stofin
was facing him.

"Aye, give up something in prayer!" several voices
urged him.

Someone pressed a bowl of *pulque* on him. Yeardance, almost seduced by the logic of these urgings,
pushed the bowl aside.

"March with me on the light-probe port of Town
Tezcatl!" he shouted at Yurl Stofin, knowing in his
heart that his plea was ludicrous. "Let's take ourselves
to the capital, that we might not be ignored any
longer!"

Cruel laughter. The bowl of *pulque* came back. He
saw his own face swimming in the milky sheen of
heartsease. No, he refused it. He absolutely refused it.
He knocked the bowl out of the other's hands. A fab-
ric of droplets at once floated up so that the image of
his face disintegrated in the air before him.

"Give up something in prayer!"

Then a pair of headlamps flashed upon the wall behind Stofin, and the kommissar turned to see the massive front end of a carrier navigating its way up the hillside between the trees. Its treads heaved it up over logs and dark-edged mounds of dirt. The world was coming, to find him celebrating the horror of Burgeontide with these other raucous muphormers. He couldn't be seen here. He couldn't let the carrier's headlamps—ravening unlidded eyes—pick him out among his confederates. . . .

"Give up something!"

Although many of the muphormers had begun to run, others were chanting at him. Someone handed him a surgical instrument, a sort of spoon. He accepted it. The crashing treads of the carrier sent their sharp echoes up and down the hillside. Its headlamps were accusations. His own eye came out of its socket easily and without pain—when it did, there were cheers and trills of ambiguous laughter. Someone steadied him. The second came as easily, and then several pairs of hands were on his back and he was running with a pack of shapes it was impossible to define except as cuffs and noises. At each jolting step his face showered away from him and a tremendous poignant ache fumbled at the limen of his awareness. The echoes of the carrier's steady grumbling were far away now, and he knew that he wasn't going to be able to go back to them.

Suddenly the hands that had been guiding him, shoving him along, were gone, and the rattles of nightfowl in the surrounding forest told him how utter was his abandonment. . . .

TWELVE

Last and First Things .

It was Gaea Zoby, wearing a pistol and picking her way along the northeastern perimeter of the Tezcatlipoca Reserve, who found the kommissar. On the second day after DeLoach and Niemiec had interrupted the muphormers' Burgeontide rites in a wood five kilometers from N'hil, the girl signed out and took up the search on her own.

Each of the civkis had done this at least once since Yeardance's disappearance, and they had purposely not reported him missing to the authorities in Town Tezcatl. DeLoach and Niemiec, after all, had sworn that it was impossible for the kommissar to be covertly forming alliances with the capital's *dingoes*.

"He's out there," DeLoach had grimly avowed, her hand sweeping out to indicate the Reserve. "We saw him run from us, you see, just as if he was one of them."

And so Gaea Zobay had gone out to find him.

He was sitting in the fork of a blackbud tree, only a meter off the ground, and the shaveskull very nearly didn't see him. He wore no tunic, and his stubble had grown into a patchy beard. His eyes, though—his eyes had been viciously gouged out.

The shock of those savage holes hit Zobay so forcibly that in an irrational reflex movement her pistol jumped into her hand and leveled its barrel on the kommissar's head. What was she doing? She brought the gun down. The tilt of the man's head made her think he was asleep—but then his head tilted quizzically to the other side.

"I hear someone," he said. He smiled distantly.

"'Sar Yeardance, how were you blinded?"

"Ah, it's my shaveskull. Gaea, go home. Let me be."

"How were you blinded, sir?" She stepped closer, with the intention of putting a hand on his ankle. "Let me take you home."

Hearing her approach through the leaf cover, he lifted his feet into the fork of the tree. "A spoon, Gaea. A spoon and a little heartsease are all you need, I think. And I *would* like to go home, you know. I really would."

"Come with me, then, sir." She put a hand up to him—a hand he couldn't see.

The kommissar drew back, the holes in his face astronomical phenomena with their own terrible gravities and spins—they seemed to suck one to destruction.

"No. Not to the Sancorage, Gaea. I'd like to go home to Jaeger. That's where I was brought up, you know." Each of his arms embraced a blackbud fork.

"Yes, sir." She wondered if he wasn't cold. Should she try to coax him down with assurances that he would one day see Jaeger again? No, she couldn't say that. Her hands were trembling. "Why did you blind yourself, sir?"

"Blind myself?" He smiled at her abstractedly, his smile not even pointing in the right direction. "A riddle."

"No, sir—"

"To put myself where I've always belonged," he

said. "To steal the sort of face I've been masking from the world for . . . for . . . Do you know how old I am, Gaea?"

"Forty-nine, you once told me, sir."

"Very well. For forty-nine years, then."

"Come down, sir. Come back with me." He had done to himself what the muphormers had been doing to one another when DeLoach and Niemiec drove their carrier into Stofin's little theater of mutilation. Perhaps he had done it then. Her colleagues had found instruments and equipment, pilfered piece by piece over the years from the Sancorage complex, littering the "altars" in the clearing. How many thefts? How many surgeries?

"Where are Stofin and his people now?" Yeardance asked suddenly.

"In the Compound again, sir. We have a number of people in the infirmary, though, and several others have come in to ask for antibiotics."

"Just like every year, come Burgeontide."

It was an indictment, insofar as the kommissar was capable of framing one. Zobay, trying to calm her hands, answered him nothing. How was she going to entice him down and return him to the admin quonset? His clotted eyes demanded treatment, just as much as did the wounds of the muphormers. His clotted eyes. His clouded mind . . .

"I want you to tell them, Gaea, that it isn't dementia. If I say it too many times even you won't believe me, but tell them it isn't insanity. Will you tell them that for me, please?"

"Yes, sir."

"The other thing is this." He tapped his head. "You see, my shaveskull, I'm still thinking. —The other thing is, I want you to tell Anscom to kidnap Stofin's child and take it somewhere where the muphormers can't put their hands on it. You tell Anscom that, do you attend?"

"To kidnap Stofin's child, sir?"

"Aye, my shaveskull. Come Burgeontide next, you see, they'll hack it out of its godhood and cease to worship it. Only perfection's worthy of worship, you know, and a new god's soon to be born. They're monotheistic, these muphormers."

"Sir, come back with me now—"

"If you don't count Xipe Totec, that is, my *nenen*." He tilted his head back. "Are the stars out? No, not likely. I feel Tonat on my hands." Singsong, he said, "*I wear my brother's skin; I wear his face. / Who am I but he? Who are You but us?*"

"You won't climb down from there, sir?"

"Not now. Is this a tall tree? I'm afraid it's too short to mount from here to Jaeger."

The girl caught her bottom lip between her teeth and bit it until blood came. Tonat was behind the man now, like a second-hand halo, and staring up at him she was blinded by its rusty light and the duplicity of her own emotions.

"Not insanity," Lucian Yeardance told her. "A joke."

She extracted from him a promise to stay where he was until she could bring back help. She ordered him to abide by his promise. She shook her finger at him while shouting, "Stay where you are, sir! Stay where you are!" Then she ran through the leaf cover, hurtling forward recklessly, and in forty minutes encountered Vowell and Niemiec in a carrier east of the Compound. But she had trouble directing her colleagues to the right tree, and when they at last found it, the kommissar was gone.

A day later the Torrentson swarm—six children moving single-file along the edge of a bog—caught sight of a bare-chested man feeling his way from tree to tree on the hill above them. The boy in the lead had a handful of brown-bottle tubers. He gave these to the ten-year-old girl behind him, who put them in a carry-bag. The six of them watched the man disappear over the edge of the hill, through a torii of white and pink blossoms. It was an hour before noon.

"Mercy," the boy said, stage-whispering the name. No one moved. The call of a bird rattled away on the wind.

"Teá, Teá-bye, Mercy," the boy said, his voice intense but not mocking. He beckoned the youngest one of their swarm forward with a hand somehow resembling a claw and put it gently on the girl's neck when she reached him.

"Farica," he said to the girl with the carry-bag, "a rock for us, I require."

Farica gave the boy a rock with a long lethal edge. He, in turn, placed this in Mercy Goron's right palm, closing her fingers over it with his own untender hand.

"It ain't for weeping and lagging back we took you on. Nor may you hope for your lopped pinky to regrow itself. Do you attend?"

The girl squinted at him. The wounds at the corners of her mouth, the shadows under her eyes, gave her the look of an old, old woman. "Aye," she said. Her voice was neither meek nor responsive.

"We took you on to do. Tubers you know, and leaf slugs, and maybe which of the barks will chew. Aye?"

Mercy Goron squinted at him.

"Mayhap it be so, little dead god. But for thirst, only

bog water and rain. Unless we do find a Dee Dum or
such to serve us otherwise."

Farica and a chunky eight-year-old boy scrabbled
part way up the hill. The other two children squatted
by the fen, staring after their swarmmates with sleepy,
red-rimmed eyes. "*Pulque*," one of them said reminis-
cently.

"He do get off," Farica said, looking down the slope
at them. "Farica fears he do get off, Holbroc."

Ignoring this, the boy spoke to Mercy Goron. "It
ain't for you to be worshiped no longer, you see. You
must *do* instead. So now we go up, and it be your call
to cut first on the maybe-priest." He turned the girl
and pushed her in the direction of Farica and the little boy beside her.

Then the six of them, Mercy Goron in the lead,
climbed the hillside, their rumps thrust out and their
hands grasping for purchase. They converged on the
torii of white and pink blossoms at the summit and
went through this natural gateway stalking their blind
kommissar.

On the afternoon of the same day, Gaea Zobay and
Anscom Niemiec went down to N'hil and found the
hut in which Womb-Beatl Stofin and her baby were
being "worshiped." The child had been Deeded to a
pair of skinmates who brightened visibly when Niemiec told them they wished to take Teo in for a new
series of tests.

"He did go with Yurl and the Radyan Maid and
Dee Dum two brace-weeks back," Womb-Beatl protested. She was suspicious. Two brace-weeks back she
might have given over the child without hesitation,
but Stofin's arrest, the kommissar's presence at the
Feast of Xipe Totec, the abrupt interruption of their

yearly rites—these things worried her. Zobay recalled one of Thordis Vowell's stories about muphormer mothers leaving their babies out for the pequia. . . .

"Nevertheless," Anscom said, "he must come with us."

And they left with the child. That was how they "kidnapped" it—one more theft in the chain of thefts linking the Sancorage and N'hil.

The kommissar was still missing. Today Ambrogiani and Vowell were out looking for him, DeLoach and Tysanjer caring for the muphormers in the infirmary. When they reached the Sancorage with the child, Anscom told the others that he and Gaea were going to take it into Town Tezcatl, to the chapter hall in which they had both been raised.

As he declared himself to the others, Gaea gathered up blankets, formula for the baby, even some of her and Anscom's personal belongings. It wasn't likely they would be permitted to come back after they had revealed to the authorities what they planned to reveal. Her heart thudded as she moved between the various quonsets, collecting and relinquishing. The spotlight in her mind hovered over the sacrifice she and her chaptermate had already committed themselves to. . . .

"I will tell Mentor Corliss," Anscom was saying when she returned to the infirmary, her arms laden, "that I fathered the child, that Gaea gave birth to it here, and that we now wish the Hall of Ahuítzotl to see it to adulthood. Mentor Corliss will see to it that we aren't treated too severely, that our story isn't too mercilessly picked at. Or so we hope."

"Insane," DeLoach said. "A muphormer baby."

"No," Anscom said. "It's not to be a muphormer, you see."

"You'll forfeit your right to go off-planet, Anse-lad,"
DeLoach said, "and our *nenen* . . . our *nenen* will
forfeit more—her apprenticeship as a star-bearer in
the Martial Arm." She looked at Gaea. "Do you understand that, Neo-starb Zobay?"

"I do."

DeLoach shook her head. "You'll wind up in Surland, Anscom, somewhere cold. And the doll will find
herself an inmate of the chapter hall for two more
years."

Tysanjer, his round face frankly unbelieving, remained silent.

"Goodbye," Anscom said. "Someone will no doubt
return the carrier."

They went outside, loaded their vehicle, and began
the long trip to the capital. The baby cried vehe-
mently for twenty or thirty minutes, soiled itself, and
didn't go to sleep until twilight. When they came
down the final slope to the lagoon plain, the wine and
silver of Town Tezcatl were almost monochromati-
cally melded in the evening darkness.

They got past the checkpoint on the Tonatiuh
Causeway only after a lengthy interview with the
guard, the summoning of several Komm-service officials, and an impromptu recorded "confession" of their
sins against the Civi-Korps ethic. Then, near midnight, the baby once again screaming, an armed escort conducted them to the Hall of Ahuítzotl. Mentor
Corliss had the infant put in the nursery.

The two young people were separated. The next
day Anscom was gone; transferred, Mentor Corliss
said, to the south.

Three days later Gaea Zobay learned the fate of the
kommissar. By a painful exertion of will she kept herself from weeping. Sorcha Corliss told her that the his-

tory of the Sancorage was being reviewed, that Governor Entrekin would have to make a judgment resolving the many discrepancies attending this affair. He was not an unfeeling man, she declared. Gaea, head down, listened with a corrosive cynicism she was appalled to discover in herself.

This passed.

One morning, in the mahogany-red dormitory where she had slept every night between the ages of seven and thirteen, Gaea put a hand on the back of her head. She was thinking about the Stofins' baby. Because it was a male child, its surname was now Niemiec. Fine. But they had given it a first name with very little forethought, calling it Skerry because its face was as round and sleek as their fellow civki's. That wouldn't do anymore. As its "mother" Gaea had an option. She was going to exercise her option. After breakfast she would go down to the nursery and tell them she had decided the child ought to be called Lucian.

Gaea took her hand away from her head. Forevermore planet-bound, she wasn't a shaveskull anymore— her hair had begun to grow.

Epilogue

It was well into autumn that Governor Darius Entrekin ordered the muphormer colony southeast of the capital abandoned and its population dispersed to hospitals, mining camps, psychological reconditioning centers, and frontier kommondorms on Surland and the Ometochtli Peninsulas.

The Long Quarantine was lifted, and a number of solitary types, their fear of muphormosy tempered by a congenital land lust, stole up into the foothills to look at the dismantled sites of N'hil and the Sancorage. The only buildings still intact were the admin quonset and the supply depot. In most cases, however, Komm-service patrols ran off the curious prospective squatters and restored the Reserve to an eerily pervasive silence. A few pequia roamed the hillsides and, every now and again, wandered into the old Sancorage feedlot to see if anyone had remembered them. No one had.

For the most part, the attempt to educate the muphormer adults to life in the larger community was a failure. Well-established prejudices operated against them, as did their own inability to adjust to so total and severe a life change. Skinmates were permitted to remain together, but otherwise the adults were separated as completely as possible. Many committed suicide. A few—initially relocated in low-security institutions in the capital, or in agrarian communes in the lake area—made short-lived escapes to their old homes. Patrols almost invariably returned them. (In the third year of the program, while trying to commandeer a lagoon fisher's canoe, Yurl Stofin was shot in the head.) As for the muphormers assigned to distant mining camps, reports indicated that they were abstracted, inefficient workers. They were religiously shunned by the adult civkis toiling in the service of Glaktik Komm, and they accepted this state as if it was a positive benediction, shying away suspiciously from any who offered them friendship. Some of these people simply ran off, never to be seen again.

So far as the authorities could determine, in thirty-five years every muphormer over the age of twenty upon Entrekin's decree had died. In the meantime, however, the struggle to accommodate them to the main thrust of Tezcatli society had been a wearing one.

The children also presented problems, but the successes here were more notable and more numerous. Once out of their "chidder swarms," the children usually went through a period of withdrawal more intense and paranoiac than their elders'. But since the muphormer system itself had required that they eventually become villagers in N'hil, there existed among the children a tenuous predisposition to accept a change of "families." They were still frequently the butt of the ingrained prejudices of the Tezcatli, however, and many subtly harassed muphormer children grew into ruined personalities with little understanding of their frustrations and rages. Others, predisposed to adapt, adapted well. The kommondorms of the Ometochtl⁵ Peninsulas, for instance, led more than twenty muphormer children into healthy and respectable adulthood.

This last fact was often noted in the investigations of what came to be known—in the medico-historiographic cadres of Glaktik Komm—as the "Sancorage Affair." Lucian Yeardance was a footnote in the investigators' preliminary reports—the last of an unbroken line of misfits and malcontents to be given the Reserve's hopeless captaincy. The true villains, most commentators agreed, were ignorance and indifference. The failure of the Tezcatli to regard the muphormers as fundamentally human was not seriously put forward as a factor in the century-long debacle. Those who argued for its inclusion in the final white paper had to admit that singling this idea out for emphasis was indeed a misleading simplification of the matter. Therefore they consented to minimize its importance.

The muphormer Feast of Xipe Totec (or so concluded most investigators of the "Sancorage Affair") had grown out of too literal a reaction to the Mesoamerican culturemongering of the colony's founder, Tiago Sciarlin—as an implementation in their own lives of the fear, revulsion, and violence with which the muphormers were met by those who had fortunately escaped the disease. The Flayed God was the perfect deity to whom to express the self-shame they felt as a result of their kinsmen's revulsion. Odious in the eyes of "healthy" Tezcatli, they became odious in their own eyes and hence ritualized their self-disgust in a yearly rite. Conveniently suggested by the Aztec mythology taught in the kommondorms as a sort of homage to Sciarlin, this rite perpetuated itself and became with the muphormers an inevitability as powerful as the turning of the seasons. If not the first outsider to observe it, Lucian Yeardance was the first outsider to participate in the Feast of the Flaying of Men. He was also the last.

Later, after the investigators had departed, the muphormer children who had obtained adulthood were asked to submit to "voluntary" sterilization. Most did. They had been raised in consonance with the Civi-Korps ethic of responsible self-denial—a variety of self-denial different only in kind from that they had accepted in their chidder swarms—and so they complied. Those who did not comply were given isolated duty-assignments, arbitrary punishments, or Komm-visas off-planet.

Sterilized or not, no matter where they might go or what might befall them, these people bore on their faces and bodies the mark of the Red Tezcatlipoca. They could not eradicate *every* trace of their origins, for the simple fact that regulations denied them access to prosthetic devices and plastic surgery. By contrast, the mark of Cain on the heads of their fellow Tezcatli was invisible.

A century after the revelations of the "Sancorage Affair," almost everyone even remotely involved with it was dead. The planet had three new frontier cities already half the size of Town Tezcatl, and other problems had arisen to occupy people's hearts and minds.